# ENFORCER

STEPHANIE HUDSON

*Emme's Enforcer*
*Lost Siren Series #4*
Copyright © 2022 Stephanie Hudson
Published by Hudson Indie Ink
www.hudsonindieink.com

This book is licensed for your personal enjoyment only.
This book may not be re-sold or given away to other people. If you would
like to share this book with another person, please purchase an additional
copy for each recipient. If you're reading this book and did not purchase
it, or it wasn't purchased for your use only, then please return to your
favourite book retailer and purchase your own copy. Thank you for
respecting the hard work of this author.
All rights reserved.
This is a work of fiction. Names, characters, places, brands, media, and
incidents are either the product of the authors imagination or are used
fictitiously. The author acknowledges the trademark status and trademark
owners of various products referred to in this work of fiction, which have
been used without permission. The publication/use of these trademarks is
not authorised, associated with, or sponsored by the trademark owners.

Emme's Enforcer/Stephanie Hudson – 1st ed.
ISBN-13 - 978-1-915118-42-4

As a huge animal lover myself, I dedicate this book to all the animal shelters and charities out there that tirelessly take care of abused, mistreated or abandoned pets and work so hard at trying to find them a new home. I was the kind of kid that brought every injured animal home to try and nurse back to health and the reason my parents came back to find two baby ducks in the bath. So, when I talk about Roger in this book, I can assure you, no cats were harmed when researching this book...

I love cats.

Roger loves no one.

# CHAPTER 1
## SELFISH SINS
### EMMELINE

P*ain.*

  That was all I felt these days.

  Pain and anger.

Both of these seemed to come in equal measure since that day. The day I realized that Raina was real. The day my perfect world came crashing down all around me and left me cut wide open and bare. Of course, I had done the very thing that Kaiden had asked me not to do but really, who could blame me?

*Who could blame me for running?*

"Take care of her! Emmeline, come back here!" Kaiden had shouted behind me, after I turned and ran. Although, where I was running to was anyone's guess, as I could barely see where I was going with the tears streaming down my face. But unsurprisingly, I didn't get far before I was caught in Kaiden's arms.

*Arms I fought against.*

"NO! Let me go! Let me go! *Just... let... me... go!"* I pleaded. I begged him to just let me go, hitting out at him

1

and pounding my small fists against his chest. And he let me. He let me do it all. But the thing he didn't let me do was leave him. No, instead he waited until all my anger had run dry and held me in his arms as I cried against him. I was heartbroken and he knew it, yet he simply held me to him and soothed my hair back, telling me softly,

"Ssshh now, just breathe... it will all be okay, Emmeline... it will be okay, just calm for me, little one." Finally, I looked up at him and through my pain, I asked him,

*"How will it be okay when my heart is broken?"* At this he clenched his jaw and before answering me, he picked me up into his arms and carried me back to our room. The moment we walked past the one we should have been going into, I felt the bitter sting of it, making me bite my lip so I wouldn't allow another sob to slip out. Because even he knew that it wasn't right anymore. That I held no claim to it any longer. Neither of us said this, but then again, *we didn't have to.*

But the part that scared me the most was when Kaiden did start speaking. Something he did after placing me on the bed. I pulled my legs to my chest and looked down at myself, seeing that I still wore nothing but his T-shirt. One I wanted to keep with me forever. I was already wondering how long its scent would last for, if I wore it every night. How long would it last once I was gone from this place?

"We will fix this... I will..."

*"Fix it?"* I questioned suspiciously, but he just kept on talking.

"I will get to the bottom of this madness and discover its true meaning."

"Its true meaning? Kaiden, don't you see, there is nothing to get to the bottom of, there is nothing left here to fix but... *but me,*" I said, forcing the painful words out and making his jaw harden as he gritted his teeth at the truth of the matter.

"No, that is not true, Emmeline, I will not hear of it!" he snapped, making me frown up at him.

"But your Siren is here now and..." I tried, but his fury erupted.

"NO!" he roared out, tearing himself from me in anger, making me cry.

"How can you say that to me! After all we have been through, after all we have shared!?" he snapped, slashing a hand out to the side when whipping back around to face me. I flinched back, now letting my head hang down at the sight of his painful reaction. Because as much as I knew it would hurt me to see him taking this any better than I was, I still knew that I had caused this. I had let him get too close. I had let him believe for too long that I could be his Siren, and now look at the damage I had caused.

I could no longer look at the evidence of my selfish sins.

The man I had wanted so badly for myself.

The man I had almost let claim me.

*"Gods, but what have I done!?"* I sobbed aloud, and this time it was Kaiden's painful intake of breath that I heard, not just my own.

"So that's it, some random woman shows up and that is all it takes for you to cast me aside and give me to her... is that it? Tell me, Emmeline, fucking look at me and TELL ME!" he roared, making me cry harder as he fought for

3

calm. Because I knew this wasn't just him saying this... *it was coming from his Demon too.*

"But she isn't just some random woman, is she? She's your Siren, Kaiden... *your Siren,*" I cried, making him growl down at me,

"No! I do not accept that... do you hear me! I do not accept that claim!" At this my head snapped up and I told him,

"But you must!"

Leaning in close, he put his fists either side of me until he was only inches from me.

"I will do no such thing, and neither will you!" I frowned in question, letting more tears fall.

"I don't understand, what...*what are you saying here?*" I asked, and the fear in my voice was easy to hear.

"What I am saying, my girl, is that this changes nothing. You are mine and therefore, you are going nowhere!" At this my mouth dropped open in utter shock.

*"You... you can't mean that!"* I hissed on a shaky breath.

"I mean every fucking word!" he growled in return, before pushing himself from the bed and turning his back to me.

"But you promised! You gave me your word!" I shouted back at him, making him snarl angrily like some wild beast,

"Then now you know that all you got from me was a lie, not my word like you thought!" At this I flinched back, as if I had been slapped.

"But... but you can't seriously expect me to stay... not now... not now there is her?" I asked, still feeling the pain of his lies like a lash against my soul.

"That is exactly what I am expecting, and if you don't

4

stay by your own free will, then you will stay solely by mine!" I started shaking my head, telling him,

"You're only saying these things because you're angry and upset."

"Gods be damned right I am! But you're a fucking fool if you believe my words to be anything other than law, because you... *Are. Going. Nowhere!*" he told me, grounding out each word and making me wince because of it.

"So I am to be your prisoner once more, is that it?" I asked wiping angrily at my tears.

"If that is what it takes, then consider this your new prison cell, for you will not be leaving it unless you are locked to my side!" I sucked in a startled breath at this and started shaking my head.

"You've lost your damn mind!" I replied.

"No, the only thing I have lost is my damn patience to have you claimed as you should have been the first fucking day I found you. *My Siren!*" he growled before storming from the room and making me run for the door just as I heard the lock slide home. Something that made me hit out against the door in vain, punching the wood until my knuckles split and my voice grew hoarse screaming for him to let me go.

*Something he didn't do.*

𐎐

Needless to say, after that it became obvious that Kaiden hadn't made the decision to keep me his prisoner because he was angry or upset. He made it because he felt as if he had no other choice. I knew this after I was woken to the feel of being lifted. Lifted into his arms from the ball I had been curled up in on the floor. He carried me back to the bed and placed me down. But the second I was free of his hold, I turned my back on him, curling up on myself once more. His deep, regrettable sigh was evidence enough how much my actions hurt him, but really, what else could he expect?!

However, as I lay facing the wall, I held myself utterly still when I felt him get in beside me. Then I was gathered in his arms and despite trying to free myself, in the end, his strength was no match for me.

*"Ssshh now, just let me hold you."* Then I felt him curse when he ran a thumb over my cut, bruised knuckles, now reprimanding me,

"You hurt yourself... this is not acceptable to me, Emmeline." I didn't speak a word, making him sigh once more in frustration.

"Promise me that you won't do this again." This was finally when I spoke, gritting out,

"Do you want my word, *like you gave me your own?*" At this he sighed again, ignoring the bite of my words, and telling me,

"I will heal this in the morning but for now, you must sleep."

"I will sleep when you leave," I told him, making him huff,

"Then we will stay awake together and let the pain of today die with the night."

*"But then what happens when the night comes back tomorrow, and the pain is still there?"* I asked in a small voice, making him squeeze me from behind.

"Then we will fight it back just the same, for we can

6

achieve anything as long as you stay in my arms." I closed my eyes at this and let the tears slip down my nose, wishing they had run dry long ago. But like my pain, I knew it wasn't that simple. Because I had tried asking for it. I had tried praying to the Gods, but they hadn't listened. Just like Kaiden hadn't listened when I pleaded with him to let me go.

There was no one in my life to listen anymore.

So, as I lay in the arms of the man I loved, I realized that for the first time in my life...

*I was truly alone.*

## CHAPTER 2
## FOOLISH HEARTS

Every night, I ended up in Kaiden's arms.
*Just like he said I would.*

Every night, he came to me and not once did the pain die with the darkness. No, instead, it just kept getting stronger. A growing despair that had me either screaming at the door or crying on the floor. And with each new night he came, he begged me to stop. Begged me to trust him, begged me to give him a chance to see for myself that I was still his Siren.

*But how could I?*

How could I, when I knew *she* existed?

Which was when I came up with a new plan. If I could just get him to see it too, then I might stand a chance at fixing this. At escaping this torture. Then perhaps I could walk away from this still living, even if it was only to live half a life without him. At least I would know that he was happy. That was all I cared about. But I knew, with me here, keeping him tethered to the wrong girl, he would never be free. He would never be free to choose his fate.

*To choose Raina.*

So, I waited for him and when he found me not in bed or upset on the floor, he was surprised. I was sitting, dressed and freshly showered on the sofa, telling him to come and sit down. He looked wary at first, as if he was waiting for me to hold a knife to his throat, one that I had stashed away again. Because yes, in a moment of weakness I had thought I could use it to threaten him to let me go.

I had kept it under the bed and when I felt him relax next to me, I jumped on him and held it to his throat.

ꭥ

*Days ago, when I threatened a Demon's life…*

My heart was pounding in my chest, something that I thought would give me away. But thinking back to every night he had come to me like this, then my heart had been pounding then too. So maybe it was just a sound he was used to. Either way, I knew this was my only chance to try and force his hand. To make him see how far my desperation had pushed me.

How far, *he had pushed me.*

So, I snaked my hand down the side of the mattress and grabbed the steak knife I had stashed there from dinner. Then with a deep breath and another moment of trying to talk myself out of this, I gripped the handle tighter and made my move.

I quickly jumped on him, pushing him flat on his back and his hands instantly went to my hips, as if this was a natural reaction. But before he could even whisper my name in question, I placed the knife at his throat. I then watched his eyes widen in surprise as the last lingering moments of sleep left him.

"Please... please don't make me hurt you... *I just want to leave. You just need to let me leave... can't you see that!?*" I told him, trying to stop my hand from shaking as I held the knife to his flesh. I knew it wouldn't kill him, because nothing like that could, but he would need the time to heal. His eyes darkened dangerously as his whole body tensed beneath me.

*"It is not wise to hold a knife to a Demon's throat, little girl,"* he warned, making me try again,

"Then that should tell you how desperate I am." He growled at that before putting more pressure on the blade's edge as he rose up, telling me,

"Then let's see just how desperate you are." But the second I saw the blade start to drip with blood I quickly threw it to one side so it couldn't cut into him anymore. Then I threw myself down on him and cried. I cried so hard, I was sobbing into his bleeding neck, telling him how sorry I was. That I never wanted to hurt him. He released a deep sigh and wrapped his arms around me, holding me tight.

*"I know, little one... I know, my Emmeline,"* he whispered as he cradled the back of my head, keeping me to him. Keeping me locked in his embrace. After that, no more was said between us but the next time I received my food...

*There wasn't a knife in sight.*

◈

The moment he entered the room and found me waiting for him on the sofa, he looked uneasy.

"I want to talk, that's all," I told him when he looked around the room as if I had some new weapon I could hold against him.

"Alright, but I warn you, if it's to beg for me to let you go again, then your hurt and pain will be felt in vain, as it won't accomplish what you want," he said, looking like he took no pleasure in it. I shrugged my shoulders at this.

"I am not asking to leave but instead, asking to stay," I told him, and he jerked back a little as if he could barely believe what I had just said.

*"Say that again,"* he uttered in shock.

"I want to stay," I told him, and I swear he looked so relieved, it hurt my heart to see. But then just to be sure, he walked closer, ready to sit next to me and said,

"You're serious, for it would be a cruelty if you jest."

"I am serious." But at this he suddenly narrowed his gaze in an untrusting way, obviously now seeing this as just another tactic of mine.

"And if you say this in hopes of gaining my trust enough that you think I will drop my guard around you so you may run…" I started shaking my head and told him,

"It is not that either, but I do have my own deal to make."

"Then the answer is no, as I already know what it is you will ask," he told me firmly after crossing his arms over his chest. And it was really difficult not to see how good his muscular arms looked stretching the material of his dark-grey T-shirt.

"But you don't even know what it is that I want," I tried again. He scoffed at this and said,

"I know enough of how your mind works, and even I can see that you are not ready to accept my claim, are you?" I sighed at this, feeling bad that I couldn't just give him what he wanted.

"No, you're right, but that doesn't mean I am not ready to make a deal and be reasonable."

"What would be reasonable, is believing me when I tell you what you mean to me, that you are my Siren… That, Emmeline, *would be reasonable.*" I closed my eyes and held back the tears at what his words did to me and instead pressed on.

"Like I said, I am ready to make a deal, and all the while I'll be fulfilling my end, I will remain here with you. So really, what have you got to lose when you have only something to gain?" When I finished asking him this question, he raised a single brow.

"And what is that?" he asked in return, which was when I took a deep breath and told him,

*"Your Siren."* He scoffed once, and stated firmly,

"I already have that."

"Then prove it," I told him, making him frown.

"What game are you playing with me this time, little Halo?" he asked, making me shrug my shoulders and tell him,

"Look, we can't keep doing this… you know you can't keep me in this room forever, I am already going crazy."

"I like your crazy," he told me, making me laugh and remind him,

"Kaiden, I held a knife to your throat not two nights ago, what do you think I will do next week?"

13

"Like I keep reminding you, I still have my chains, pet of mine," he said, and I could tell he was only half joking.

"Yes, well before we both enter the realms of sex slave, crazy fucked up relationship, let's be real here." At this his eyes deepened, and I could tell his mind was still lingering on the sex slave part of that sentence. So, I slapped the back of my hand to his arm and said,

"Focus here, big boy." He chuckled at this and looked down at his own lap, where I could see now the very large bulge straining against denim, before telling me,

"Stop putting sexual thoughts in my mind where there is already many and I might focus better, sweetheart." I chuckled at that and before I could stop myself, I patted his crotch and said,

"Down boy." At this he snatched my hand up in his and growled low, making me flinch back. Then he raised my hand to his mouth and started to bite on my fingers, making me moan.

"Tease me, Emmeline, and you will discover very quickly where it gets you and much to my disappointment, I believe it is the very last place you want to find yourself these days." Then he finished this warning by looking back towards the bed, making me quickly snatch my hand back.

"I'm sorry, I don't know what came over me... I... you're right... I shouldn't have done that," I stammered out before he took pity on me, seeing the way I was struggling here.

"You never need to apologize for touching me, little Halo, as you will find these days, not only do I crave it, but I miss it. I mourn what you have taken from me... I mourn your touch, little one," he said, and I closed my eyes tight as his words made my chest ache again. I even felt the tears trying to claw their way to the surface. And he knew. He knew what it was he did to me, which was why he said,

"You said let's be real, so go back to telling me what being real means to you, exactly?" I took a deep breath and told him the part of my plan he would hate the most.

"I want you to date Raina." At this I got the reaction I knew I would, as he rose to his feet and told me,

"Then you are already at that fucked up stage of crazy if you think I will…"

"Look, just hear me out," I interrupted quickly, making him growl down at me,

"No, I will not sully how I feel for you by entertaining this fucked up idea of…!"

"I want you to pick me, okay!" I snapped, quickly rising to my feet and making him take pause.

*"Come again?"* he whispered, asking me this time in a way as though he thought he hadn't heard me correctly.

"I want you to give us both a chance, spend time with both of us and then by the end of it, if you pick me, then I will know you're doing it because you truly do believe I am your Siren and not because you never gave who could be your real Siren a single chance," I told him, getting it all out quickly, knowing his reaction would be shock all the same.

"Then let me save you the time and myself the trouble, you are my Siren and I pick you!" I closed my eyes for a moment and tried again.

"And what of Raina?"

*"What about her!?"* He all but snarled, making me flinch.

"Have you spent any time with her?" I asked, hating how hard that question was to ask.

"Of course not!" he snapped, making me feel guilty that I had a moment to feel glad about that, even if it was defeating the object of what I was trying to achieve. But that didn't stop my irrational mind from questioning every second of my day, if he was in fact spending time with her... and now... *well, I knew.*

"Look, I get that this is hard on both of us, but I can't do this with you unless I know for certain," I said, making him growl,

*"Know what?!"*

"That's she isn't your Siren," I replied with the obvious, something he clearly wasn't getting here as he threw back,

"She is not!"

"But how do you truly know that, if you haven't even spent time with her?" I said trying for reason and pushing my point across hoping it would stick... needless to say, *that it didn't.*

"Because I am staring at my Siren right now!" he roared, making me wince.

"But how do you know for sure, how do any of us know for sure?" I continued, as surely, someone here had to give. Something I said would have to start sticking soon... wouldn't it? Now I wasn't so sure as he seemed determined, perhaps I was foolish thinking that he would be willing to give this a try. I knew that the moment he narrowed his gaze down at me.

"So what, you want me to fucking date another woman just to be sure I will pick you at the end?" he snapped, making me release a sigh and tell him,

"Yeah, pretty much."

"That is fucked up!" he snapped, making me cringe back again.

"But…"

"But nothing! I refuse!" At this I closed my eyes and when he stormed to the door, he told me,

"I will leave you to your crazy fucked up ideas of what it means to be someone's Siren, for clearly, you're not the expert you thought you were. Maybe a night alone is what you need to clear your foolish head of this madness!"

And with that he left. Left me alone and crying.

Left me alone with…

*My Foolish Heart.*

# CHAPTER 3
## HURT
### WRATH

I stormed from the room knowing that if I didn't leave when I had, she would now be having the rest of this fucked up conversation dealing with my Demon! For I wasn't the only one furious beyond all reasoning. Hence why, as soon as I made it to my office, I grabbed the nearest thing to hand and threw it across the room. It hit the panelled wall and exploded into tiny shards of pottery as though it had been detonated.

"Not that I give a shit, but I do believe that was a Qianlong Dynasty Vase," Hel stated from the doorway, and I growled,

"I don't give a shit if it was carved by Jesus!" This made him laugh, which was the last fucking thing on my agenda.

"I take it things still aren't going well?" His calm tone made me growl sarcastically,

"Oh, what gives you that fucking impression, brother?"

"Well, your office is becoming more sparce by the day and any time you don't spend in it, you spend trying to kill people in the training room... *myself included.*" He muttered this last part, rubbing his jaw as if remembering when I dislocated it a few days ago from throwing a mean punch in the ring.

"How fucking perceptive of you!" I snapped, and he released a sigh before walking fully inside, closing the door behind him, making me snap,

"Oh, fucking save it, Helmer!" At this he held up his hands in surrender and said,

"I haven't said anything yet."

"Yes, but if it is another voice of reason I don't need, didn't ask for or wont fucking listen to, then you can leave now," I told him, making him sigh.

"How about a brother willing to just listen, you got time for that?" he threw back, making me exhale before deflating in to my chair and feeling like a shit, as he was right. He had only ever tried to help despite feeling far beyond it. But even I had to admit, this was a new one, even for my little Siren, a girl who had held a blade to my neck in her desperation to be freed.

A painful memory and one that admittedly, wouldn't fucking leave me. But I knew she hadn't had it in her to hurt me, as she had freaked out the second she saw me pressing myself against the blade, nicking my skin. She had thrown the measly weapon and buried her head in my neck, sobbing in her guilt.

*And I had held her through my own.*

A guilt I had fought against the moment she saw that woman and ran from me. The moment I had kept her as my captive ever since. It damn near killed me every time I saw her cry. Every time I found her curled up in so much pain, so did my heartache increase. All of it felt in vain for if she would only trust me, then I could solve this pain. If she would only trust in my words when I told her she was mine. Because I knew it. I felt it with every beat of my heart. With every breath I took, she was mine.

Which was why I couldn't let her go.

I just couldn't.

*My Demon wouldn't let me.*

I had tried to explain this to her. I had tried to explain so many things, but she wouldn't listen, and I just didn't know how I was ever to make it through to her mind with my feelings. There just didn't seem to be enough words to say and if there were, then I didn't know them. But then looking at her, and I knew each day she was pushed more to breaking point.

*We both were.*

I just didn't know how to fix it. For the first time in my entire existence, I was at a loss at what to do. I knew I was hurting her. I knew she felt betrayed by a promise I made. One that I never imagined I would have to fulfil, as I knew without a shadow of a doubt who she was to me. Which meant there was no way I was letting her go, that was not something I had ever consciously promised. Not when she was my Siren, not this other woman, *not this Raina!*

I just wished that she knew it too. Which was why I had felt hope for the first time in days when walking in that room today. Especially when I found her looking composed, and for once that haunted look was gone. Her red eyes were back to big, bright, swirls of chocolate brown. They had hope and life in them once more.

Now I knew why, I thought bitterly.

"So come on, out with it. What happened this time?" Hel

asked, making me grit my teeth at just the thought of her utterly absurd request. I watched as he walked further inside and leant his weight back against the side of the brown leather couch, using its large square armrest to place his hands upon. I released a heavy weighted sigh and dragged a hand down my face, as if this would help in clearing my head.

"More tears, I gather," my brother said, obviously trying to prompt me for an answer. Because he knew it all, as I had been at a loss at what to do, needing my brother's council more than ever, despite often claiming the opposite.

"No, for once I would have taken the tears over pure madness," I said bitterly, surprising my brother.

"Jeez, that bad huh?"

"What she now suggests is beyond my comprehension," I said, throwing up my hands and letting them fall as fists on my desk.

"How so?" he asked, making me shake my head before giving him this new level of Hell I found myself dealing with.

"She wants me to date this other woman." At this Hel coughed a laugh before saying,

"Excuse me?"

"You heard me right, I told you, it's madness," I said, making him frown in a questioning way, a look on my brother I knew to be wary around. Helmer was planning something.

"There must be more to it than that… what aren't you telling me?" I raised a brow, making him add,

"I know my brother, Kai, that is not all she said, as she must have given her reasons."

"Oh, she gave them alright," I muttered with a grimace.

"Fuck, brother, this is like trying to get blood from the Devil!" I sighed before admitting the root of her insane request.

"From my understanding of it, she wants me to date this other woman, spending time with both of them and then once I am sure, her hope is that I pick her," I told him, shrugging, but he clapped his hands and said,

"Excellent! I hope you told her yes." At this I jerked a little in my response to this, shaking my head before asking incredulously,

*"Excuse me?"*

"This is fucking perfect!" he added with a smirk I wanted to dislocate again.

"How the fuck is this perfect?!" I snapped, making him roll his eyes at me as if he was dealing with a freaking idiot.

"Let me get this straight, the girl you're in love with, the one you believe more than anything is your Siren, just gave you a perfect way to eradicate her fears once and for all, and you took this as bad news?" I narrowed my gaze and he slapped himself upside the head and groaned.

"Gods help me, you blew up at her again, didn't you?"

"I am at a loss to know how this is a good thing, Hel," I snapped, ignoring his exhausted tone.

"And I am at loss at understand how you could fuck up an offer like this," he countered, making me growl,

"An offer? Fuck that, dating another fucking woman I don't give a shit about is not what I would call a fucking offer!"

"Exactly! A woman you don't give a fucking shit about, and the woman you do care for is asking you to spend time

23

with her so she can be one hundred percent certain that you don't care. Gods, brother, but she wants you to pick her, something you can do and finally you two can get on with your lives together, you can claim her and we can all start getting back to fucking normal and beating the shit out of people we want to kill," Hel said, throwing this all at me like it was as easy as fucking pie!

"You're actually saying that I should entertain this shit?" I asked, wondering if I should be surprised that he would see this as a good thing.

"No, what I'm saying is, you should quickly run back in there and take her up on it before she realizes the fucking lucky hand she just dealt you!"

*"I can't believe this..."* I muttered to myself with a shake of my head.

"Yes, the feeling is mutual," he replied dryly.

"I am not in the fucking mood here, Helmer, so just..."

"Act rational, sure thing, brother, and I will start by going and telling the girl that you have changed your mind and will do as she asks," he said, walking towards the door when suddenly I was up out of my seat.

"You will do no such thing!" I barked.

"Answer me something, Kai, what is the worst that could happen?" he asked, making me lose a little wind out of my argument when I took a minute to try and think of something. Oh, and my brother didn't miss it, releasing a sigh before telling me,

"Look, all Emmeline wants is proof that she is your Siren and that won't happen until the summer solstice. Not unless you figure out another way to prove it to her and well, brother, she just gave you one." I frowned at this as I hated

24

to admit, some of what my brother said was starting to hold weight.

"So, you think I should be agreeing to this?" I questioned again.

"Fuck, yeah!" he said on a laugh before he took my glare as a sign to drop being a cocky shit for five seconds.

"Look, I get it, spending time with another woman is going to drive your Demon insane, but if that is the worst of it, then isn't it worth it when in the end you can tell her without any doubt that this Raina isn't your Siren? Because that is all she wants, you know," he added, this time with a little more compassion for my frayed nerves.

"Yes, she all but said as much," I admitted.

"And you ignored that part, didn't you?" I groaned at this and scrubbed a hand down my face, making him chuckle.

"Fuck off!" I snapped, and he laughed harder this time.

"I know you, brother, you gave this idea of hers not a single second of thought but instead, only saw it as another fucking hoop she wants you to jump through, when all you want to do is…"

"Burn, kill and destroy every fucking hoop and obstacle in our way and fucking claim my Siren!" I growled, making my brother grin.

"Yeah, when all she wants is to do right by you and make sure you're choosing the right girl… trust me on this, brother, the girl loves you and feels as if she is sacrificing what she wants most in this world for the sake of your soul," he said, making me suck back a breath.

"And you know this how?" I asked, and he granted me a sympathetic look.

"Anyone with half a brain can see it, you just need to

25

know when to look," he told me, making me turn my face away in annoyance.

"Tell me, Kai, what do you see when you look at her?" he asked, now standing before me on the other side of my desk, placing his hands on the wood. I sighed and told him the truth.

"I see…" I paused, not knowing if I could allow myself to spill these kinds of emotions, even in front of my brother.

"You see…?" he prompted, and suddenly, anger made me stand, and I was telling him exactly what I saw in Emmeline without holding back.

"I see everything, alright! I see a life of happiness, I see my very reason for breathing, doing so for love, when I once thought it was all for Wrath. I see the keeper of my soul and the reason it feels like my heart actually fucking beats! I see my eternity, Helmer…" I took a deep shuddering breath and told him…

*"…I see my Siren."*

## CHAPTER 4
## BARGAIN TO STRIKE

fter admitting this heartfelt admission, I was left staring at my brother, feeling as if my Demon was going to burst out of my skin without first being let out of its mental cage. Because as much as a being like myself was at one with my Demon, I also knew that to allow it too much control was a dangerous thing. To maintain dominance over that other side of yourself was crucial, or it would take over completely and rule not just your vessel but more importantly, your mind.

*Becoming rogue for a Son of Wrath was not an option.*

Which was why I needed to be careful with all these new emotions, especially the ones that pushed at my Demon to take control. His need to take over and claim what we both knew was our Siren was riding me harder and harder each day. Hel would know this, hence his driving need to want to help me.

He knew how I struggled... *how I suffered.*

"Come on, brother, like I said, what is the worst that can happen here?" he asked again.

"This could backfire, and I could end up breeding more strength in her doubt," I admitted because this was my fear... *my only fear*.

"You find the girl begging you to let her leave and she held a knife to your throat no more than two nights ago, and you think this is going to make that worse? What next...? Taking away her spoons at dinner time?"

"Not amusing, Hel," I growled, but he ignored me and carried on.

"Or you could eradicate her doubt once and for all... besides, this is also a chance for you to strike a bargain."

*"Another bargain,"* I muttered, remembering my first bargain made with her on the plane... *another of my brother's ideas*.

"Yes, one that benefits you, because if she wants you to spend time with this other woman, then it stands to reason that you should get to spend just as much time with her in return, even more I would say." Now this was finally the part I started to entertain.

"I see you like this part," he commented with a smirk.

"It is the only part I do fucking like." Hel laughed at this before agreeing.

"Then it seems you have some negotiations to conduct." I finally grinned at this before telling him,

"As for this Raina, I want Franklin to continue looking into her background." My brother agreed, telling me,

"Of course, we will keep digging, but spending more time with her will give you a good opportunity to discover these things for yourself, as you might actually have an enemy on your hands this time." I rubbed a hand across the back of my neck at that, already feeling my Demon growling at me at the very idea of spending time with another female.

"An interrogation that would certainly go far differently than my time with Emmeline, that is for fucking certain." At this he laughed again and said,

"Yeah, well I doubt she would start singing Mambo number fucking five, that's for sure... *funny girl.*" He added this last part muttering to himself and shaking his head, as if he still found the memory amusing. I had to admit, having listened to the song myself since that day, then I had to agree with him... *my girl is funny.*

"It was most definitely resourceful," I agreed with a grin, one my brother mirrored.

"Fuck yeah, it was, and from the sounds of it, she hasn't stopped being resourceful either." I sighed at this.

"I guess not," I muttered, thinking that she was clearly trying to find a way to resolve this and now having time to think about it, I knew that I had reacted badly.

"Then what the fuck are you still doing here?" My brother pointed out, making me smirk before placing my hands on my desk to stand, then leaning forward I told him,

"You're right, I have some negotiations to start, and I know the perfect way of getting what I want," I said, pushing from my chair and walking towards the window, instead of towards the door like my brother expected.

"What are you up to, brother?" Hel asked, making me laugh once.

"I believe that's usually my line." He scoffed at this before it clicked.

"You want me to go get her, don't you?" I turned side on

29

to look at him, leaving the view of the perfectly manicured gardens beyond.

"Makes sense, seeing as this is usually where business is conducted," I replied, making him chuckle and comment knowingly,

"And it offers a more intimidating setting."

"I believe it's time to bring my girl out of her little comfort zone and back into my world," I confessed, making my brother smirk.

"Now there is the ruthless brother I know and love." At this I joined him in his sinister grin, matching his for one of my own. Then I told him,

"It's time to see if I can't make my Siren sing once more." At this he left the room chuckling, and for the first time in days, I felt my Demon ease and not fight me for control. As I had a plan and this time, I wasn't going to let my Siren's fears get in the way of getting what I wanted.

I would finally get to claim my Girl.

One way or another.

The moment I heard her knocking on my door I grinned to myself. However, I remained facing the window with my arms folded when I called out,

"Come in."

"Erm… Hel said you wanted to see me?" The moment her tentative, unsure voice spoke, I felt my Demon rumbling inside of me, as was his usual response to our girl. I swear he had learned how to fucking purr since meeting her!

"Yes, come in, Emmeline," I said, purposely keeping my voice steady, and even somewhat stern, knowing I would need it to aid me in getting what I wanted. I glanced over my shoulder, seeing that she was still standing by the door, fidgeting nervously, and I had to suppress a grin at how fucking cute she looked.

A pair of indigo leggings, a strappy white top under an overly large, and a sweater the colour of teal was the same outfit I had seen her in earlier. The knitted sweater also had a large hood that kept making it slip from one shoulder but was one she kept wrapped around herself with a brown belt. As for her hair, it was as I preferred it, down in a wild halo of blonde curls around her head. I just wanted to bury my fist in it. As usual, she was wearing heels and today's choice was a pair of brown boots, a sight that again had me forcing back a smirk. Because I quickly realized something about my little Siren, and that was that she had a thing about her height. And well, being only five feet tall, then it didn't take a genius to guess that it was clear she wanted to be taller. Not that I got to see this shorter height often, as like I said, she was rarely seen without heels. As for my own preference, I fucking loved how little she was, and loved how curvy she was even more. It just made my hands itch to touch her, and any chance I got I was picking her up or throwing her over my shoulder. Just the feel of her sitting in my lap brought me a sense of peace of the likes I had never known, nor was it a sense I'd believed I needed. But my Demon calmed in such a way I had experienced before. Just the feel of her touch and I swear, he was like a fucking puppy rolling over and showing her its belly.

That was how much power she held. Not that she had any fucking clue, like now. How much strength it took just to hold back from striding over to her and taking possession of her lips, telling her without words the only thing she needed to know...

*The strength of my heart... one she owned.*

"You may close the door now," I added, trying to prompt her to come further inside as she looked like she wanted bolt from the room any second. I heard her whispered little sigh from the other side of the room as she closed the door. But because I wanted to follow through with my plan of intimidation, I purposely locked the door, making her jump a little at the sound.

"Take a seat... if you please," I said, nodding to the chair opposite my desk and adding this last part when she didn't move. Gods, but she looked like a rabbit caught in headlights. I purposely turned back to the window, so she would find her bravery to do as I asked, without me watching her. Then I gave it another moment of silence between us once I heard her shifting her chair back after taking a seat.

"I have been thinking about your ideas on how we can move past this," I said, now turning to face her and catching as her head snapped up, forcing her to brush her wild curls back. I had to force myself not to grin at the endearing sight.

"You have?!" she asked in a hopeful tone.

"I have, but you should know, Emmeline, I have conditions of my own." At this she slumped back in her chair, tossed up her slim hands and muttered,

*"Of course, you do."* I had to suppress a laugh at this. Fuck, but I had to suppress a lot of things.

Like picking her up and kissing her.
Kissing her and proving just how well made…

*My desk was.*

## CHAPTER 5
# NEGOTIATIONS
### EMMELINE

The moment Hel turned up and knocked on the door, I knew he was there on behalf of his brother. But of course he was, as he had, no doubt, been the one to deal with his brother's rage. Gods, Kaiden had been so angry at me even suggesting that he spend time with her. But then, what else was I supposed to do, as I knew we couldn't carry on as we were?

"So, are you here to tell me I'm crazy too?" I asked from where I still sat on the couch, wiping away my tears angrily.

"No, that would be the wrong brother, sweetheart," he teased with an easy smile that I knew, one of these days, a girl wouldn't be able to resist, making me wonder if he too was destined for a Siren? It was one of the things I always wondered about him, but seeing as it wasn't something I ever dreamt about, then I had never written it into any of my books. Which meant that I just didn't know.

"So, you agree with me?" I asked feeling hopeful, knowing that if I had Hel on my side, that would count for something. Actually, it would count for a hell of a lot, seeing as Hel was the only person Kaiden ever seemed to listen to.

"I do, which is why you'd best come with me, while I have Kai in that same mindset," he told me, making me quickly shoot to my feet.

"You do?!" I asked enthusiastically, making him chuckle.

"Oh come on, Emmeline, did you really doubt that I could?" I laughed at this and walked over to him so I could pat his arm, telling him,

"Didn't doubt you for a second." At this he smirked, bowing his head as if he was touched.

"Then, shall we?" He offered me his arm and I couldn't help but slip my own in his, before telling him,

"Well, it beats being held over the edge of a balcony any day."

"Ouch, I was waiting for that to come and bite me in the ass." I laughed at this and told him as we left the room,

"Yeah, well I knew what I was getting into the second I stepped inside your club and lucky for you, I am a forgiving soul." He chuckled at this and said,

"Then I would say it's lucky for my brother also, as I have no doubt you will need that forgiving soul... and often." I giggled this time, making him grin down at me. After this we walked in comfortable silence before stopping not far from what I assumed to be Kaiden's office on the second floor. I had to admit, it wasn't a place I was yet used to seeing, never having dreamt much about it. Hel pulled me back before we reached the office and told me,

"Do me a favour and go easy on him, yeah? He's..." he paused to look at the door and finished his sentence, *"...he's struggling with all of this."* After this he left me standing outside and I looked to the door, thinking on his words. Then after I raised my hand to knock about three times, I finally followed through with it, jumping a little when I heard his deep voice telling me I could go in.

After this I had to wonder if what Hel had said was right, because it seemed more fitting for him to have given this advice to his brother. It didn't look like Kaiden was going to make this easy for me. I knew that, the moment I found him standing by the window with his back to me. I even swallowed hard when I saw the way his T-shirt strained across the impressive muscles on his back due to having his arms crossed.

*Gods, but he looked so formidable.*

But two minutes later, and even after he told me that he had been giving thought to my idea, I knew when he told me he had conditions of his own, that it wasn't going to be as straight forward as I had hoped. Maybe this was why Hel had asked me to go easy on him, had he known what Kaiden would want from me in return? Gods, but I was being a fool, as knowing Hel, it would have been his idea!

"So these conditions of yours...?" I let my question linger, and knew it was a bad sign when he finally turned around to face me and smirked.

"You want me to date this other woman, take time to get to know her... is that right?" He repeated my idea, and I warily agreed, having first forced myself not to react the way I wanted to. Which was to cringe at the idea of it myself. However, I pushed myself to remain neutral and said,

"Raina. Yes, I want you to give it a chance so you can be

sure what it is you want by the end of all this." He too looked to force calm as he nodded his head, but the clenched fists at his sides told me a different story.

"Then my only demand is that however much time I spend with her, I spend double the amount with you," he told me, and my mouth dropped.

"But that's too much!" I protested.

"This is not including the nights you continue to spend sleeping in my arms," he added, ignoring my outburst and walking over towards me. I would have got up out of the chair, but it felt too late, as I was quickly trapped as he cut the space between us too swiftly.

"Kaiden, be reasonable here…" He was anything but, as he suddenly placed his hands either side of the armrests, caging me in before telling me,

"Do you want me to talk to you about the difference between reasonable and realistic?" I shook my head telling him no, making my hair bounce around my face. His eyes darkened at the sight before he reached out and tucked a few curls behind my ear as he often did.

"You wrote about my Demon, Emmeline, therefore I shouldn't need to remind you what would happen should I be forced to be without my Siren for too long… it would be, should we say… *dangerous.*" I shivered at this, especially the way he growled the last word.

"But that shouldn't happen if you spend more time with Raina," I tried, making him narrow his gaze down at me for a second before leaning closer and whispering in my ear this time,

*"And what if you're wrong?"* I couldn't help but shudder

at this, knowing this time a simple shiver wasn't going to cut it. Then he gave me some space, pushing back from his hold on the chair and instead leaning back against his desk right in front of me.

"I am not willing to take that chance, not when my Demon is already pushing at me to claim you," he said sternly, making me swallow hard before asking,

*"What... what do you mean?"*

"It's simple really, he already believes, *as I do*... that you are our Siren and until we finalize that fact in the bedroom, then his frustration and impatience will only grow..." I quickly tried to interrupt him,

"But what if..." He never let me finish.

"We are already restless when not with you and now, you want to add another reason in the mix to piss us off?"

I stammered at this, "But... but... Raina...she could be..." The second I heard wood splintering in his hold I stopped, seeing now the way his hands had started to turn into those belonging to his Demon, telling me he was not exaggerating here.

"What do you think will happen if you push us even further by taking yourself out the picture for even longer, for I am telling you, this is playing with fire, Emmeline," he warned, making me release a heavy sigh.

"I am just trying to do right by you here," I admitted, making him take a breath and force his hands back to that of his vessel. I knew then that he had been trying to prove a point and let's just say, it was one I heard loud and clear.

"Then start by listening and making your decisions based on what is best for the both of us and in turn, I will try and do the same," he replied, and this time I got the softer side of Kaiden.

"So, you will spend time with Raina?" I asked, making him nod in agreement, and I knew then that it was the best I could hope to get at this point. Although that didn't stop me from trying for more.

"I will, as long as I spend double the amount with you in return," he said, making sure I was accepting his own terms.

"Okay, fine, but it has to be for a month." At this he laughed once and said,

"I will give you a week, little Halo, and no more."

"A week!" I shrieked, getting to my feet this time, only before I could put too much distance between us, he reached out quickly and snagged the end of my belt, using it to tug me closer to him. I gasped in surprise and as I tried to pull back, he yanked harder, making me go stumbling into him. He growled low in his chest, and I felt it vibrate against my palms I held at his chest.

*"I believe we have been here before, little one,"* he whispered down at me, and I tried so hard not to let his sexy, rumbled words affect me... needless to say, *trying was pointless.*

"Please, you have to give me something here," I told him, making him yank at my belt suddenly, and this time it was to undo it. Then before I could stop him, my belt was gone, and tossed to the floor. He then separated the two sides of my cardigan and was soon framing my waist with his big hands. After this I let out a little yelp when he picked me up and turned with me in his grasp. I felt my bum hit the top of his desk and before I could stop him, he was stepping closer, spreading my thighs wide to give him enough room. A second later and he growled down at me,

"This is what I am going to give you, and I advise you listen and listen good, beautiful… this between us…" he paused so he could drag his heated gaze up my body, framing my sides with his hands before stroking his way up. Doing so until his thumbs were grazing the underneath of my breasts, making me gasp.

"It's as real as it gets and it took me all of two minutes in the interrogation room to know who you were to me… so trust me when I say, *a week is more than enough, Halo.*" I shuddered as he squeezed me tighter when he said this last part, and I closed my eyes against the intensity of his gaze.

"And this?" I asked, needing to know if acting this way now would be the last time during that week or not.

"If you're asking me if this is the last time I am to touch you this way, then you clearly haven't been listening, sweetheart," he told me, getting even closer and to the point that I lost his eyes. Because I was too scared to tip my head all the way back and find them again. So instead, I focused on his chest and the way the material stretched tight across the muscles every time he took a breath.

"But surely you can understand how that makes it harder, to know that you will be like this with us both." At this he scoffed, and I hated how much I was relieved to hear what he said next.

"If you think I could be this way with anyone else but you, then you need reminding of…" He paused, and I finally looked up and asked in an unsure voice,

*"Of what?"* He narrowed his gaze for half a second

before suddenly, his hand was fisted in my curls and he was growling over my lips,

*"Of this!"*

Then I gasped as he slipped his tongue inside, and my heart started to beat faster for him once more as he...

*Kissed me.*

## CHAPTER 6
# TEARS IN BLOOD

*ods, how I had missed his kiss.*

The moment I felt him grab my hips and tug me closer to the edge of the desk, I gasped. A move that ended up fitting my core in a more snug position against his hard length. A shockingly large erection that was no doubt straining uncomfortably against his jeans. That was when I knew I needed to stop this. But of course, this was easier said than done, seeing as I let out a blissful moan as he created that perfect friction against my clit.

"Fuck, woman, but if only you would just let yourself be mine and give yourself to me... *the deliciously wicked things I crave to do to you,*" his husky voice whispered in my ear and along with the dirty image he painted, well, it was enough to have me gripping onto his shoulders, holding myself to him. Even though I knew I should have been trying to restrain him back, I just couldn't seem to help it. I wanted him more than anything in my whole life and up until a nearly a week ago, I could have had him.

*I had been so close.*

But then, like always, the sight of Raina standing in that hallway entered my mind and it was like dousing my arousal in ice cold water.

*"Kaiden, I..."* The moment I said his name he growled possessively, and I knew it to be a turned-on sound, as he quickly took ownership of my mouth, kissing me breathless once more. It was as if he was addicted to the taste of me, and when his hands pulled down my cardigan, I knew I needed to break this connection before I ended up naked on his desk.

"Kaiden, please, we need... we need to... to stop." His growl this time sounded more aggressive, as if his Demon was the one denying me even a single moment free of his lips. I knew this when he left my open mouth and started biting my neck. It was as if he was trying to deepen the marks he had made there when I first arrived. Of course, they were starting to fade now, and I knew that he didn't like the sight of me without his bite, which was obvious every time I caught him looking. If truth be told...

*I didn't like it either.*

"Kaiden, honey, please... *please don't make me regret making this deal with you,"* I said, and his growl turned into one of frustration as he rested his forehead to my neck, now breathing me in deep as he tried to calm himself. I couldn't stop myself from comforting him, raising a hand to the back of his neck and stroking the heated skin there. The deep rumbling sound was one I could feel vibrating against my hand and neck.

"That helps as much as it doesn't," he grumbled, and the

second I stopped, he chuckled before taking that same hand in his and bringing it to his lips to kiss.

"Alright, Emmeline, we will play this your way."

"Thank you… this… well, it means a lot and I want you to know that," I told him, because it did, but then this led me back on to my main concern, and that was the broken promises he had given me once before.

"Ask it of me, little one," he said, reading the concern in my eyes. So, I took a deep breath, knowing this was where his sweetness would most likely end.

"You're not going to like it," I warned, making him scoff.

"Why am I not surprised?" I gave him a wry look, making him chuckle.

"I will try and behave, now ask me," he said again.

"I need to know what happens to me, should you… erm… *choose her.*" At this he froze, and quickly his head was back in my neck, taking hold of my flesh as if his Demon had been the one to answer me, and it was nothing short of a warning. Of course, he didn't break the skin, but it made me cry out before telling him quickly,

"Look, I get that you don't want to think like that, but I have a life too. I deserve to know what's going to happen to it should the worst possible outcome happen to me… *please Kaiden*, please try and understand my fears." I pleaded with him and before long, he was kissing the slight sting. And once again, just like the first time in that interrogation room, I was getting turned on by it.

"Regardless of the outcome, you will be taken care of… of that you can be certain," he told me against my abused skin, running his nose up his bite, one I knew from the strength of it, would be left there for another week at least. Which was precisely what he wanted. I was sure of it. I pulled back at this and told him,

"Okay, so just as long as we are on the same page here, I don't want your money or a house or whatever mega rich idea you might have had in your head." At this he raised a brow, one I ignored and continued on.

"I just want back what I had, that's it... I don't need anything more." Now at this he narrowed his eyes and told me in a stern tone,

"Not that this is a conversation we need to be having right now, but just so you know, you will never go back to that." Honestly, he had practically growled this, as if making it a law or something.

"Kaiden." I said his name in exasperation, something he promptly ignored.

"No! I will not hear of it and unless you want to call this deal off and I send this Raina as far away as humanly possible, then I suggest you accept this as being an absolute." I released a frustrated sigh and gave up by snapping,

*"Fine!"* He had the audacity to smirk at this.

"Now, can you please let me off the desk?" I snapped, making him fight a grin before he took a step back and made a show of holding out his arm as if to say, 'be my guest'. I slid off and was looking around for my belt after pulling my cardigan back over my shoulders, when he cleared his throat.

"Looking for this?" he said, making me look to see it dangling from his fingers. But the second I tried to take it, he simply held it higher, making a 'tut, tut' sound.

"What do I get out of it?" he asked, clearly enjoying himself, making me fold my arms across my chest before replying,

"To continue to walk around like you haven't been kicked in the balls?" He laughed at my witty response, telling me,

"You may try and when you fail, I will take you down to my training room and show you how it is done properly." At this I scoffed and said,

"Do I get to practice on you?"

His badass grin added to his answer. "No, Tristan."

I laughed at this, knowing that he was joking and when I thought he wasn't paying attention, I lunged for my belt, but again, he was too quick for me.

"Grrr! Give it back!" I shouted in pretend irritation, because really, I was enjoying the game.

"You growl like a kitten, it's cute." I rolled my eyes at this, making him chuckle.

"Do it again, I want to hear it some more," he teased as I glared at him.

"Do you want to see my claws too?" I said, making him growl a little but this time, I knew it was in a playful manner. Then he snapped out my belt to the side and with a flick of his wrist, he had it caught around me. Then after quickly grabbing the other end, he used the leather to draw me closer, tugging me into him.

*"I would prefer your teeth,"* he told me, growling again, and I frowned in question before he told me,

"Bite me and you get your belt back."

"What! I can't bite you!" I almost shrieked, making him grin mischievously.

47

"Why not? I bite you all the time," he said, running his nose along my latest mark, making me shiver.

"Why do you want me to bite you?" I asked, making him tighten his hold on me. Then he said one of the loveliest things I had ever heard said to me.

"Because if I have to spend time with this other woman, then I wish to do so with a piece of you on me. So that when I struggle, I simply have to reach up and touch the piece of you on my skin... *that my, little Halo, is why.*"

I swear, nothing would have been able to help my reaction, as I grabbed his T-shirt in my fist and started to tug him over to the sofa.

"What are you playing at now, little one?" he asked with a smirk, allowing me to lead him.

"I'm getting my belt back," I said, reaching up and snapping my teeth at him, making him grin. Then I made a point of taking the belt from him and throwing it across the room, making him chuckle with a shake of his head. Then, as I got him where I wanted him, he asked,

"Is that so?" His tone was teasing, even with its growl of words making me grin.

"No, not really... now sit your ass down, big man," I said, making him roar with laughter this time as I pushed him down to sit. Then I did something stupid, something deliciously stupid. I straddled his waist, putting me at the right height. His hands instantly framed my hips, making me tut at him this time.

"Tut, tut, hands off, Kaiden Wrath," I ordered, making him growl at me.

"My rules this time. Now, no touching," I told him, and his growl turned into a groan making me giggle.

"I see you're enjoying yourself when bossing me around," he complained half-heartedly.

"But of course," I said, winking at him and making his hands tighten on my hips before I granted him a reprimanding look in return.

*"And they call me a sadist."* He grumbled this muttered complaint under his breath before doing as I asked and let me go. Again, his comment made me chuckle. And yet, despite knowing that I shouldn't be doing any of this, I couldn't seem to help myself. Like when I kissed his nose and said in my sweetest voice,

*"Good boy."* Again, he grumbled, and I glanced at his hands that had turned into fists, no doubt to stop himself from grabbing me again. I bit my lip at that to stop myself from smiling.

"Now, hold still," I warned before kissing my way up his neck, making him moan in a hoarse way that had me beaming against his skin that smelled divine. He was all man, and I swear I nearly lost my damn mind, wanting to taste every inch of him. Oh yeah, this was a bad idea alright, I knew that. But damn, it was like waving the sweetest, tastiest lollypop in front of a sugar addict! Which was why my kisses turned into licks of my tongue before I sucked gently at his flesh.

"Gods, woman, have mercy and cease your teasing tongue," he growled, and once again my grin was one he could feel against his skin. Then I sucked some more, licking up the length before sucking again, making him caution,

"Little Halo, be warned, I am getting closer to my limit here." This time I started kissing and the second he snarled my name,

49

*"Emmeline!"* I suddenly bit down hard on his flesh, doing so with enough pressure that it would have hurt anyone else. But not Wrath, as the second I tasted his blood, I was suddenly in his arms, and I was falling backwards. However, he twisted our bodies quickly, so instead of landing on the floor, I landed with my back on the sofa, with him on top of me.

Oh yeah, *this had been a bad idea.*

My mouth left his flesh as I cried out in shock, making him growl down at me,

"Now bite me harder!"

"I can't, I don't want to hurt you," I told him, making him snarl,

"Harder, girl!" Then he cupped the back of my head and pushed it back to where he now bled a little. So, knowing that I had stepped well beyond the point of no return, I did as he asked, marvelling at how drinking down his blood made me feel. I would have thought the act distasteful and coppery, but it wasn't. I even moaned as I bit down harder, feeling more blood seeping out of my teeth marks, making me suck him down. But with every hard pull on his blood I took, the more his body tensed above me, holding me so tight, I could only just breathe through it. Gods, but it was one of the most erotic moments of my life and I forced myself not to look too closely into questioning why.

I only knew that in my moment of madness, I wrapped my legs around him and started rubbing against the hard length of him, rocking myself along his cock.

"Fuck yes, drink... drink, my girl, drink from the blood you own," he told me as I rubbed my clit faster and faster against the bulge in his jeans, building my pleasure as I sucked him down harder. Then, after one last bite down, my hardest yet and feeling my teeth sink in even further, he suddenly roared. He reared back, making me lose my hold on him, as I too cried out my orgasm. I felt the bulge in his jeans grow damp, knowing then that I hadn't been the only one to find my sexual release. It took me back to our time in his office, and the moment he came down from his high, I knew I wasn't the only one whose mind had taken them down memory lane.

"Soon, there will be nothing between us and I will get to empty myself inside of you like I fucking crave to do." He panted out his words. Words that were gravelly and hoarse, telling me how close he had come to damning another promise and claiming me regardless. Gods, but half of me had wanted him to and, man, if that didn't just make me feel like shit. Because I wasn't helping this situation.

*No, I was making it worse.*

But then why couldn't I seem to help it?

Because I fucking loved him, that's why!

However, I didn't tell him this. No, instead I tried to ease the tension of my mistake by teasing him.

"Looks like I got more than just my belt back." This worked as he started laughing, at the same time he gathered me up in his arms and held me to him. Of course, I couldn't help but hug him back, hiding my tears and forcing them to stay where they were. Because as much as I knew I should have regretted this, I just couldn't find it in my heart to do so. And that caused me even more guilt to torture myself over. But it was my guilt to carry and mine alone, which was why I did my best to hide these feelings from Kaiden.

To hide my emotions and to hide…

*My tears in his blood.*

# CHAPTER 7
## FIRST DATES

I had to say, I was getting tired of cursing myself, and this self-sacrificing act that was admittedly tearing my heart apart. After this slip-up in the office, which I had let get totally out of hand, I had excused myself quickly, needing to put space between us. Something I knew he hadn't wanted to let me do, but then I guess he took one look at my face and knew not to push it. After all, he had got his bite, something I knew meant something to him. This was proven when I saw him later that day, and I was shocked to see that he hadn't let it heal like he did every other injury he sustained.

No, *he wanted this to leave a scar.*

I knew it when he walked inside the room and was dressed ready for his date. Something that would have been significantly more painful had I not asked him about it...

◈

*Hours earlier...*

53

"You look nice," I commented, trying to hold back the ache at seeing him dressed smartly, knowing it wasn't for me this time. And really, which girl could ever resist him in his dark grey jeans and a black shirt worn moulded to his large muscles? It was also one he wore as he usually did, without a tie and rolled up to his forearms. Oh, and I wasn't even going to get into the smell of him, hating for once how irresistible it was. He even had his favourite leather jacket in his hand, something he tossed over a chair when he first entered.

Gods, it was almost too painful to even look at him. Which I think he could tell, as he sighed once before closing the door and walking further inside, only stopping when he was within touching distance of me. I knew this the moment he lifted my chin up so I could no longer hide my eyes by staring at the floor.

"Then I have achieved my only goal by gaining your compliment as it's the only one I will ever look for." I couldn't help but grin at this, making him say,

"Make that a second goal." This was referring to my smile, I knew that when he ran his thumb across my lips. Which was when my eyes noticed his neck and I couldn't help but ask in shock,

"It's still red and sore?"

"But of course, I would never rid myself of your mark."

I opened my mouth in shock, and the pad of his thumb slipped in for only a second as his eyes heated looking down at me. I came so close to pulling it the rest of the way in and sucking on it, when I stopped the impulse. Because I knew it would just be asking for delicious trouble, the type that only Kaiden would be able to give me. And he knew it too, because he chuckled once before leaving my lips and instead caressing his fingers down my neck to my own bite mark.

"I am going to have Hel bring you to the club to meet me there," he told me and I tried not to wince, knowing where he was going first.

"So, tonight is the first... erm... date then?" I hated myself for asking and his look said it all before his words followed.

"There is still time for you to put an end to this before it even begins, you merely need to say the words, Emmeline... *you merely need to tell me you will be mine and let me claim you.*" He said this last part by framing my waist and pulling me closer. I sucked in a shuddered breath before forcing myself to do the right thing, telling him,

"Have fun getting to know her." At this he scoffed.

"Doubtful, but I have promised to try, and that is all I am willing to do," he replied, making this somewhat easier for me. Gods, but I was so torn! Torn with wanting him for myself and trying to do what was right by not denying him a chance at knowing his true Siren. Which was why he had to give this a chance.

*We both did.*

Later that night, I found myself in 53 Sins, trying to force myself to relax and stop looking at the fucking door for more than two Gods be damned minutes! Even Hel had chuckled at me the first few times I did this, making me scowl at him. Although, after about two hours of this, he finally took pity on me, looking up from the screen on his phone long enough to tell me,

"Don't worry, my brother won't be much longer now."

"I'm not worried," I said quickly, making Hel chuckle,

"Yeah, so that label is just offensive to you, is it?" he asked, nodding to the water bottle in my hands that was now minus the label as I had unconsciously scratched it off.

"Didn't anyone ever tell you, it's not nice to be a know it all," I replied, making him smirk then rub his chiselled jawline in a comical way as if he was giving it some more thought.

"I can't remember, perhaps someone did once but then his neck was most likely under my boot," he replied, making those on his council snigger. I rolled my eyes but then forgot this the second I noticed that the people in the VIP all seemed to move as one. Everyone seemed to sit up straighter, shifting a little closer to the table as all eyes turned towards the doors.

As for myself, I tensed and my heart started to pound faster as I sensed Kaiden's return, turning to look and taking a quick breath when I found him searching for me. Then, after seeing him grin to himself, he continued to walk with purpose towards us. Gods, but he looked utterly gorgeous, with those long legs striding towards me and those badass tattoos on show. Painted skin that moved as he flexed his muscles as if the sight of my defiance was making him itch to get to me sooner.

Because I hadn't done as I had been told to do.

"You are not sitting where you were supposed to be sitting," Kaiden informed me, now towering over me and making Hel grant me one of those know it all looks. This was because when we arrived, Hel informed me that his brother had requested I sit in Kaiden's spot while he was gone. But I had taken one look at his throne-style chair in the centre and told him firmly,

56

"Absolutely not."

Because I knew this was Kaiden's way of making a statement, one I was definitely not ready for him to make. So I had declined and taken a seat off to the side, putting Hel in between me and that chair.

"I thought it best to…"

"Defy me, *yes I know,*" he finished for me, and before I could defend my actions I was being plucked right out of my seat, making me yelp. Then, before I could get my bearings, I found myself positioned in his lap and held there with his heavy arm now banded around my waist.

"Finally feel better, brother?" Hel asked with a knowing grin, and the moment I felt Kaiden's arm snake up the front of me and stroke a finger down my jaw, he answered,

*"Most definitely."* I swallowed hard, trying not to let myself put too much into his words, but feeling the warmth from them all the same.

"Kaiden, I don't think…"

"You look beautiful tonight," he interrupted, taking the wind out of my defences as I was just about to argue against sitting here.

"Oh… thank you… I'm erm… glad you like it," I said, referring to my dress and brushing my hands down the silk. It had a babydoll cut, with a skirt which flared out around my knees, thanks to its layers and layers of material. The top part was a halter-neck style, wrapping around my neck with a big floppy silk bow at the back. It was also black lace, with big roses attached to sheer skin material that looked invisible and therefore showed off hints of my own bare skin beneath the design. A thin strip of black ribbon separated the plain from the fancy, matching the ribbon on my strappy sandals.

As for my hair, I had twisted it off to one side, purposely keeping my new bite on show, as I knew this would please him. I had taken some time on my make-up, trying to create that seductive smoky look. One I admittedly had to look up a tutorial online for to achieve.

*"I would like it better adorning my bedroom floor,"* he whispered seductively in my ear, making me sigh back against him, having no other power than to just whisper his name,

*"Kaiden."*

"Yes, Emmeline?" he asked, purposely purring my name.

"Gods, but you're not going to make this easy for me, are you?" I asked, making him answer instantly,

"I never said that I would. But then, with such temptation at my fingertips, I would remind you, that for me, *you make this even less so."* I gasped when he ran his fingers up my thigh, gathering the silk as he went. This made me quickly grab his wrist, trying to stop him from going too far.

"Bumblebee pyjamas tomorrow night it is then," I said, making him chuckle before growling in my ear,

"That doesn't make it any less tempting, sweetheart." I blushed at this.

"Blow up sumo suit it is then," I joked again, making him laugh louder this time. But then he purposely held up a hand in front of me and with a click of his fingers, his whole hand changed into that of his Demon. I sucked in a quick breath, jerking back a little at just seeing those dangerous, wicked looking black talons, connected by rock hard scaled skin.

"I hear they are quite easy to cut into, like slicing open a fig to get to its sweetness at the centre." I rolled my lips inwards to stop myself from giggling and this time, went for something else.

"Fine, a medieval knight it is… you don't happen to have any chainmail lying around this place, do you?" I teased, making him roar with laughter before telling me,

"Like a hot blade through butter," he said, making a swiping motion with his claws before clicking his fingers once more before his mortal hand came back.

"It makes no difference, nothing would save you from my hunger to taste your skin." He finished this by proving his point as he sucked on the latest mark he had made on my neck, making me moan.

"You don't play fair, Kaiden," I only half complained, making him smirk against my tender skin.

"Like I said, I never intended to, as you know what I want." I sighed, letting my head fall back against his chest before telling him,

"One date is not enough." He growled a little before the next words he told me shot straight to my heart.

As he rumbled his reply in my ear…

*"It was for me."*

# CHAPTER 8
# LEATHER JACKETS

"*It was for me.*"

I had no words to this, as anything I said in that moment would have been saying too much. So instead, I took hold of his hand and squeezed it, hoping this was enough to let him know how much his words had meant to me. But as his words played over and over, I realized that I needed some time to compose myself. Because I knew that I would have ended up doing something I regretted... like throwing myself at him and begging him to take me back to his home... or more specifically...

*His room.*

"I need to go to the bathroom," I said, suddenly letting go of his hand and trying to get up from his lap. Thankfully, he got the hint and let me go, making me stand quickly.

"Emmeline?" He said my name, getting to his feet himself and when I refused to look at him, he gripped my chin and forced the issue. However, whatever he saw in my eyes must have made his decision for him, especially after I told him in a quiet voice,

*"I need to pee."* He narrowed his eyes for a second before a tenderness came over him, causing him to nod down at me.

"Alright, little Halo. Boaz, if you please." Kaiden finished by gesturing to his second in command. Obviously, this told me that he would only trust those closest to him with my care, and that only included those in his inner circle. It was no doubt why, on our way here, I was not only in the car driven by Hel, but it included an escort by four other cars filled with his men, making me feel like some first lady or something.

Boaz stood, making Kaiden say,

"Can you show my girl here to the bathroom?"

"But of course, my Lord Wrath," was his answer, and as I walked away, I heard Kaiden stop him and say,

"Stay outside the door and stand guard." I wasn't sure whether this was for my benefit of safety or if he was ensuring I didn't run. Not that I could blame him for not trusting me, as I had told him not long ago that I would run the first chance I got. And well...

*That hadn't changed.*

"This way, Miss Raidne," Boaz said, holding his arm out and glaring at anyone who even looked our way.

"Thank you, and please call me Emme," I replied after he held the door open for me. He bowed his head and told me,

"If my Lord Wrath permits it, then I will." I grinned to myself at this. He looked like some exotic biker, dressed in his casual ripped jeans, a worn biker tee under a checked black and grey shirt, with his dark, wavy blonde hair tied back. But it was his tanned skin and his almond-shaped, light-brown eyes that had me wondering at his origins.

Needless to say, he was ruggedly handsome, despite knowing that he was one of the meanest Demons around and had been with Wrath for most of his second life.

He led me back into the lobby area and after first checking the bathroom was empty, he held the door open for me to go inside. I thanked him and the moment I was inside, and the door was closed, I went straight over to the sinks. Then with both hands holding the sides, I let my head hang down for a few seconds before looking up at myself and asking aloud,

"What are you doing, Emme?" I shook my head before turning around and using the toilet, looking down at my fancy underwear, asking myself what the point of a thong was. Hell, no girl wore cheese wire unless they thought someone would see them or the tight outfit required it.

*I had neither excuse.*

And what was with taking longer doing my make up this time or taking the extra time shaving the bits I knew no one would see?

"Because your inner hussy has hope, that's why," I told myself with another shake of my head. Gods, but could I be anymore torn, hating how much his words affected me? I had been so happy to hear he had wanted to get back to me. To hear how one date had been enough, despite knowing myself that it wouldn't be. Because he could still be confused about how he felt about me and that could be enough to prevent him from giving Raina a chance.

Did I really want her to have one?

Yes.

No.

Fuck!

I released a deep, pained sigh, focusing instead on washing my hands and not about the night ahead where I knew it would end as it always did…

*In Kaiden's arms.*

These were shamefully the moments I looked forward to the most, even though I knew it was wrong. Even though I was still hurt he had broken his promise. Even though I was glad that he had.

*Even though I had no rights to him.*

Not like Raina did.

"Pull it together, girl," I said to myself after washing my hands and shaking them a little before finding a hand towel. Then, after taking a deep breath, I walked out of there with a new mindset, to try not to encourage Kaiden to act like my boyfriend. Although admittedly, how well I was going to achieve this was anyone's guess, as ever since the interrogation room, he hadn't stop touching me. Not once. Maybe I should just go with the flow and stop overthinking things…

*Stop overthinking, Raina.*

Something that would have been easier to achieve had I not turned a corner and ran straight into the one fated to be Kaiden's. Boaz had tried to save me, holding me steady from behind as a heel caught to the side. Whereas for Raina, she was…

Painfully stunning.

She was tall, slim, and I swear it looked as if she lived in the gym as she was toned everywhere. There were no squishy bits, like I had on my hips or where my belly had a tendency to find itself over my knicker-line. No, she wore her red dress like a damn model, a cut that would never have suited me, as it was a sheath style, finishing just above the knee. Even her hair shone as if she had her personal sun following her around to shine down on it, making it look like spun gold. A style that was so unlike my own, it was almost funny, seeing as if I wanted to achieve the same look, I would have to rely on one of my wigs!

She wore it clipped to one side with a stylish, glittering clip clustered with red crystals. This matched her red pouting lips and blushing high cheekbones. I swear she had the type of face that would have made Leonardo DaVinci weep before begging her to pose for him to paint.

And most of all, I knew that she had the face... *that was deserving of Kaiden's attention.*

"Oh, I am so sorry, I heard footsteps and thought it might be Kai, as I just wanted to give him his jacket back. I was cold and well, he was such a gentleman," she said, ending this in that sing song laugh of hers, and I felt every word she said like a knife to my heart. He had been a gentleman to her. But of course, he had. He wasn't an asshole. And she called him Kai... *but of course she did.*

Gods, I was such a fool.

"No problem, I will make sure he gets it," I said, taking it off her and seeing it was his leather jacket from before. *His favourite leather jacket.* And the very same one I had first seen him wearing in the elevator. The one he looked utterly gorgeous in. Okay, stop Emme, just stop it!

"Wait, you must be Emmeline... right?" she asked, with her light blue eyes looking me up and down, smiling, but I could tell there was an undercurrent of something... *something ugly.* But then if he had mentioned me, and she was his fated, then could I really be surprised? She most likely had no idea I had written about her. That I had once felt as if she was another friend of mine. That I had been just as close to her as I had to Kaiden when writing my books. But that was before I had ever met him, knowing no one could take that claim.

No one was closer to me than Kaiden.

*Not now.*

"Yep, that's me," I said, trying to sound upbeat when all I wanted to do was run a fucking mile and not stop until I was on the next plane out of here.

"You're the one who wrote to me, the reason I finally realized all these dreams I had been having were real, that Kai was real... thank you!" she said, suddenly grabbing me to her and pulling me in for a hug. Boaz quickly intervened, trying to gently separate us.

"It's okay, Boaz," I tried to say, shocked by her warm reaction to me, which was when I realized why... Kaiden hadn't told her who I was to him. Because he couldn't have. Not when she was reacting this way to me. I would be lying if I said that it didn't hurt.

It hurt a lot.

But then I couldn't be surprised, as what was he supposed to say, that I was his Siren? No, he couldn't have said that, not when the whole point of this was to find out *who she was to him.*

"I'm not permitted to allow anyone to touch you. Please step away, Miss," he said, making her respond with a little,

"Oh, of course." I mouthed a silently, 'sorry' in return, making her smile.

"Anyway, if you can tell Kai that I had a wonderful time and look forward to our next date, then I would be grateful."

I tried not to wince at this. No, instead, I acted my most calm self and swallowed hard before nodding. Then I muttered a strained,

"Sure thing... will do." After this I started walking, needing to get away from her and quickly, before I started crying, something I could feel myself close to doing. However, as soon as I was out of sight, I stopped walking, looked up at the ceiling and closed my eyes.

"Miss?" I held a finger up when Boaz no doubt wanted to know why I was acting crazy, so I added,

"Just need a minute here." At this he released a sigh but other than that, he didn't say anything more, he just waited.

"You can do this... You can do this... man up, Emme," I muttered to myself, making Boaz ask,

"Man up?"

"Just ignore me, it's called the shittiest pep talk in the world... right, I'm fine now, let's go," I said, making him chuckle softly behind me as I started walking, forcing myself to act normal. He then held the door open for me and totally surprised me when he told me,

*"You've got this, girl."* I swear I would have hugged him if it wouldn't have looked suspicious. Instead, I nodded my head like a crazy lady, biting my lip to stop myself from crying, something he looked as if he knew I was close to doing. So, he motioned me to go in, and the second I did, it was as though Kaiden felt it, as he instantly looked my way. Honestly, his grin nearly broke me!

I just wanted this night to be over. Damn it, I just wanted a place I could go and hide. A place I could breathe without his scent wrapping itself around me. I just needed sanctuary against his touch. But the second he was standing, I knew there was no chance of this. However, the moment I came further into view, his gaze homed straight in on the jacket I carried. This was also when his grin was quickly replaced first by shock and then by annoyance.

He looked straight to Boaz, who didn't say anything, but I looked back in time to find him shaking his head a little. So, with nothing more to do but put on my best performance, I grinned up at him and passed him the jacket,

"I just bumped into Raina, she seems so nice, which is great. She's great. Really! Anyway, she wanted me to give you this, asked me to hand it back, so here it is... your jacket. So, what does a girl have to do to get a drink around here? Huh?" Then I grabbed his whisky and downed it back in one, just to shut myself up.

"Whoa, easy, sweetheart," Kaiden said, taking the bottle from me as I had just poured myself another one... *a large one.*

*"Looks like someone needed that,"* Hel commented dryly, making his brother growl at him. Then he took the glass from me and placed it down slowly, before taking me in his arms.

"Emmeline, are you okay?" he asked, making me look anywhere but directly at him, really wishing he wouldn't ask me that. It was the kiss of death for my tears.

*"I am fine...* just tired that's all, can we go soon?" I asked, hating how squeaky the first part sounded.

"Hey, look at me," he pressed.

"I said I'm fine, just need another drink, that's all... maybe I should go the bar. Hey, does anyone else want one?" I asked, scanning his council who were all looking a little concerned, but I ignored this and said,

"No? Okay, just me then." Then I started to walk away, but Kaiden only let me take one step before he was reaching out and taking me in his hands.

"Hold up, beautiful, you're not going anywhere until you look at me."

"I said I am fine, geez," I said in a strained voice he didn't miss.

"Emmeline, *look at me now!*" he ordered, more sternly this time, making me finally give in and look up at him, hating that it took only seconds before tears filled my eyes. It also took him less than that to realise I was far from okay as he whispered my name tenderly,

*"Oh, little Halo."*

I swallowed hard and started shaking my head erratically, pleading with him without words.

"Alright, sweetheart…" He paused, and suddenly I was safe in his arms as he picked me up and cradled me to his chest. Then he said the only thing I needed to hear in that moment…

*"Let's get you out of here."*

# CHAPTER 9
# PAINFUL REALITY
## WRATH

I knew this was a bad idea. Scrap that, it was the worst fucking idea I had ever agreed to. And here in my arms was the fucking proof of that! Because, at the first moment Emmeline had encountered Raina, she was now trying everything in her power not to cry. And the only reason I was not breaking things in my rage was because I had my fragile girl in my arms.

Gods, but just seeing the pain in her big chocolate brown eyes looking up at me, trying to be brave and keep it all in, well, it broke my fucking heart! But I hadn't been lying when I told her that one date was enough, as I knew Raina wasn't the girl for me.

*She wasn't my Siren.*

Yet, what I hadn't said was how, despite this knowledge, I had strangely felt drawn to her. But like I said, I couldn't really understand why. I was putting it down to the girl acting very similar to the way Emmeline had written her in the book, which admittedly, made me question fucking everything!

71

I also didn't want Emmeline knowing, but after spending time with Raina, I couldn't help but be worried. Because despite needing my time with her to be awful, unfortunately I couldn't claim it had been. Of course, I would have much preferred to be with my little Halo but as for my Demon, he had felt strangely at peace with Raina also. I also started to overlook the fact that she was not my type and even though it made me a bastard, I did find myself often comparing the two.

Needless to say, Emmeline won every fucking time of course. But even the fact that I was doing so was enough to concern me, especially with the way my Demon reacted. Although, it also had to be said that the moment I had Emmeline back in my arms was when my Demon really settled. The differences were most definitely noticeable. For there was still no doubt in our minds that Emmeline was our Siren.

Now I just needed to convince her of that.

Something made infinitely harder when she was meeting Raina for the first time and being told how much of a fucking gentleman I was! Damn it, but I'd had no clue at the time how much offering her my jacket when she had been cold would hurt my Siren. But then I had told her we would be going to the roof garden for a drink and would she not feel better with a jacket of her own. She had assured me she would be fine, laughing and cursing herself when ten minutes later and she was shivering next to me.

Of course, I wasn't enough of a bastard that I would let the girl go cold but still, placing my jacket upon her shoulders had felt... *wrong.* And now I knew why. Because Boaz had offered up his memories of the exchange to me, adding Emmeline's reaction. It was a memory that had me clenching my jaw, as just seeing for myself the way she tried to calm her emotions before walking back into the club was painful enough. Gods, but it was beyond fucked up and again, had I not wanted to break another promise to Emmeline, then I would have called an end to this whole fucking thing the second I picked her up in my arms.

*Just one week.*

That was all I had to do until she could be mine. Until she could trust me enough to make that claim and know that I meant it. But as for now, well I wished I had the right words to say to ease her suffering, knowing how torn she was. I was no fool, I knew how the girl felt for me, and it was that love that was the driving force behind this crazy decision. Because she wanted me to have my Siren. She wanted that fate for me, more than even her own happiness. How could I be angry at that? How could I be angry about that level of devotion, at that depth of love?

*I couldn't.*

I could only try and understand it.

So, I carried her from my club and gave her the time she needed to gather her own thoughts. And while I did this, I took comfort in how she gripped her delicate fist in my shirt and rested her head on my shoulder. This meant that in turn, I could breathe her in deep, taking in the beautiful scent of her hair.

But then we got to my car, and I felt her tense, doing so in a way I suspected it was because she didn't want me to let her go. *I hoped it was this.*

"If I didn't already know it would scare the shit out of you, I would offer to hold you while I fly us home," I told her, making her laugh, telling me her emotions were still riding her hard.

"Yeah, not sure raining vomit is a great look, although seemed like an apt way to end the night." I scoffed at this.

"The night is not over yet, for my favourite part is still yet to come," I told her as I let her legs go, so she could stand. But then, as she looked up at me with those big eyes of hers and asked,

"What part is that?" I grinned down at her, and I couldn't help but tuck her curls behind her ear before telling her,

"Where I get to sleep with you in my arms all night." At this she closed her eyes and let her head fall to my chest, whispering my name like the sweetest prayer.

*"Oh, Kaiden."*

❀

I knew something was wrong the moment my Siren started to stir in my arms as it seemed as if she was having a nightmare. I had got her home as quickly as humanly possible. Without scaring the shit out of her with my manic driving nor the use of my wings. But I had felt a pressing need to get her as far away from Raina as I could, and I didn't need to be a genius like my brother to understand the reasons why.

"Ssshh now, I am here," I cooed down at her, trying to offer her restless mind some comfort, when suddenly she cried out, piercing the night along with my heart.

"Emmeline!" I shouted her name, wanting her to wake and break free the hold her nightmare had on her. At this she started thrashing in the bed, and I had a job to try and contain her, fearful that she would hurt herself.

"No! No, get off me! Kaiden help! Help me please!" she screamed, and I swear I felt her desperation like a knife in the gut!

"Wake up! Emmeline, wake up... NOW!" I roared this last part, doing so in a Demonic voice that made me shake.

"AHHHH!" She screamed louder this time, and then tried to bolt upright out of my arms, something I wouldn't allow. Then she finally woke, panting for breath through her desperate, fearful tears.

"Kaiden, Kaiden... I... can't..." She started to panic so I turned her to face me, and took hold of her, framing her pretty face with my large hands. Then I put my forehead to hers and told her softly,

"Ssshh now, you're safe, just breathe... *just breathe with me.*" I started to take in slow, steady breaths, getting her to do the same.

"That's it, easy now... that's it, good girl," I told her, until finally she was calm enough that she threw her arms around my neck and clung onto me. It was as if I had the power to keep her safe from even that of her own mind. But in that moment, I had never cursed my inability to be able to access her thoughts. I couldn't understand why I couldn't, or that none of my kind could. Not when Ward's Siren was an open fucking book to us all. Something he took great amusement in, for she certainly had a quirky personality. Someone I had come to meet when saving her after her own Enforcer Ward was unable to do so, due to hunting down the bastard that took her from him.

She was also a good and pure soul, just like my own

.Siren, and someone I was very much looking forward to introducing Emmeline to. I knew they would most likely form a strong bond. But right now, I focused on my own Siren, and that included questioning what she had been dreaming of and how it was best to help her.

*"Kaiden."* She whispered my name as if this helped to anchor her to reality, and every time she said my name this way, I felt it heating up my entire being. As if there was some unknown switch buried deep at my core that only she had the power to turn on.

*She warmed my soul.*

*"I am here, my Halo, I am here,"* I whispered back, stroking her hair and holding her to me so she would feel safe... so that I felt reassured, *she was safe.*

"I had a bad dream," she told me after a few silent minutes looking at me and making me chuckle softly.

"Yes, I know, Halo."

"I'm sorry I woke you," she said thoughtfully, making me shake my head at her before pulling her in for another hug, cupping the back of her head, holding her to me.

"Never apologize for that, my sweet girl, as I am thankful I woke and could save you from your nightmare." At this she squeezed me tighter and I knew my words affected her. She usually did this when I said something that touched her heart, whether it was a squeeze of my hand or the way she whispered my name. It was reactions like this that I had become addicted to, along with everything else about her. Gods, but if someone had told me this was how I would be, then I wouldn't have fucking believed them!

I would have been a foolish asshole.

"Do you want to tell me about it?" I asked, making sure

to keep my tone gentle yet coaxing, as I wanted to know what had troubled her so.

"I was at the club, and I was walking outside into the street when suddenly, men were there. They tried to take me, and I was fighting them... I was... *trying to get back to you."* She added this last part in a whisper and the irony wasn't lost on either of us, I was sure. Especially, seeing as she had been trying to do the very opposite since I had taken her prisoner weeks ago. Fuck, but she had run from me, managing to escape me once... *never again!*

"It was just a dream, for I would never let any harm come to you... *I would never allow anyone even the chance to take you from me."* I growled this last part, telling her without words what would happen should anyone even fucking try! She shivered, no doubt feeling mixed emotions to that deadly statement, and I held her tighter in response.

But then, just as I was going to suggest that she lay down and relax back into sleep, I tensed, feeling my brother's emotions as if they were my very own. For we were connected, my brother and I... *we always had been.* Which was how I knew, seconds before he knocked on the door, that he was running towards this room.

"Come in, Hel!" I shouted before he had chance to raise his fist to the door, walking straight inside instead. Emmeline tensed in my hold and tried to pull back, something I wouldn't allow as I held her tighter against me.

"Kai, I need..."

"Just tell me, for I keep nothing from my Siren," I stated, knowing it would go a long way in making her feel as important to me as she was. I wanted to prove this fact. My brother sighed and told me what felt like the impossible after what Emmeline had just experienced.

"It's Raina." I tensed at that and didn't have long to wonder how my girl would take my reaction.

"What happened?" I asked in what I knew was a stern, pissed off tone.

"Is she alright?" Emmeline asked, and I had to admire her concern, for if I had been in the same situation, any other man in Emmeline's life I found myself contending with, well, they would have found themselves dead long ago. Simple as that.

"She was attacked." Emmeline gasped, letting her hands fly to her mouth while I growled in annoyance.

"She is fine but naturally shaken up," Hel said, but this time it was Emmeline's question that beat my own, asking it as if she already knew the answer.

"Where did this happen?" I held my breath and let it out again when my Demon growled the second he said the impossible.

"Outside Lexington…" he paused, before continuing on with Emmeline's own nightmare…

*"…They tried to grab her off the street."*

## CHAPTER 10
# GONE GIRL LOST

Naturally, after my brother said this, I was up out of bed and excusing myself, asking for Emmeline to wait for me. As I knew now that this was one conversation, I didn't want to have in front of her.

"How did this happen?" I asked the moment I was in my office, dressed and not where I wanted to fucking be. No, I wanted to be naked with my girl, skin to skin, falling sleep with the scent of her hair drifting up my nose. *Not dealing with this shit.*

"Tristan was shadowing her, like you instructed, and some assholes turned up trying to drag her into their car, talking about finding your Siren and using her as bait."

*"Fuck!"* I hissed, just thankful that it hadn't been my actual Siren they had almost snatched from me.

"Yeah, my sentiments exactly," Hel agreed with gritted teeth.

"Tell me I at least have some fucker to interrogate?" I snarled my words in my anger.

"Unfortunately not. Tristan left little more than body parts after his own rage took over." This was not surprising, as Tristan was two ends of the spectrum. Being laid back and relaxed most days but if his Demon had need to be released, then he was one hard motherfucker that would spare no one.

"Where is she now, was she harmed?" I asked, making him give me a pointed look.

"Don't give me that fucking look," I added in annoyance, making him shrug his shoulders.

"Do you blame me, not long ago you wanted me to ship the girl off to somewhere in Australia, with a fucking pay off to disappear." This was unfortunately true, something my brother refused to do as he knew Emmeline would have had a fit over it, should she ever find out. And considering her invested interest in the girl, then there was little doubt that I would have been unable to keep that knowledge from her.

"Just answer the fucking question, Helmer." He rolled his eyes but then told me,

"No, like I said, she was just shaken up and last I checked, asleep in her new room."

"New room?" I asked, having a bad feeling about what he would say next.

"I had no choice, Kai." I scrubbed a hand down my face and sighed.

"Please tell me she isn't fucking here."

"You know security is better here, and Hell, since Emmeline, Greenburgh is nothing short of a fucking fortress after the fucking army of guards you had brought in," Hel pointed out, making me groan this time before snapping my own point back,

"Yeah, but that was mainly to stop her from getting out!"

"Well, now it's to stop any fuckers from getting in... look, I get this isn't ideal..." Hel tried again.

"Not one Gods-be-damned thing is fucking ideal here, Hel, most of all, having them both staying under the same roof. After all, there was a reason I had Raina staying in one of the apartments at Lexington," I reminded him.

"I get that, but she is adamant," my brother said, making me frown.

"She is?" I asked having a bad feeling in my gut.

"She said that she doesn't feel safe not being where you are." I groaned at this.

"And what am I supposed to tell Emmeline? She is already fucking struggling with this!" I barked, hating this whole fucked up thing!

"Yeah, I know, I was there, brother. The whole fucking council knows it... shit, never heard Boaz asking after another person in my whole life, let alone showing concern." This made me growl before my brother snapped,

"As a friend! Fuck, no need to go trying to tear his fucking head off, he just cares about your queen... we all do, Kai."

"Yes, well that better fucking be the extent of it!" I growled, making him roll his eyes again.

"More to the point, do you want to tell me what all the screaming was about I heard coming down the hallway before I got to your new room?" Hel asked, making me wince.

"She had a nightmare," I admitted, knowing what was coming next, or more to the point, what I would have to divulge next.

"Sleeping with you, she would," he joked, making me rumble my annoyed reply,

"If only it was about me, and not the premonition it was."

"Okay, so you're going to have to explain that one," Hel scoffed.

"She had a dream that she was being taken outside of Lexington, men trying to grab her," I told him, knowing what his response would be before he gave it.

*"You're shitting me!"*

"No, trust me, I wish I fucking was!" I retorted feeling the tension in my neck mounting. I needed my girl's hands on me, rubbing the strain away with her touch. But fuck me, I swear her touch was fucking magic!

"So, she is connected to the girl?" my brother asked, making me tense.

*"Don't,"* I advised through gritted teeth.

"What?" he asked, knowing full well what!

"Don't fucking go there, Helmer," I warned again, making him sigh this time.

"Well, whether I go there or not, it does not change the fact that decisions need to be made. So, what do you want to do here, Kai?" I leaned back against my desk and held the bridge of my nose in frustration.

"Fuck if I know."

"In that case, may I suggest keeping her here for the time being, as it will give us both a chance to watch her more closely. I still haven't ruled out the possibility of her being here for nefarious reasons. She may still prove to be our enemy," Hel said, as he was usually the most distrusting one out of the two of us.

"Just as she may prove not to be," I countered.

"Well, that is a bridge you can cross when your seven days are up."

"Six," I corrected, making him laugh.

"Six whole days with two women who both want you to claim them... fuck, good luck is all I will say, for I still have my bets on them trying to kill each other over you."

I growled at that.

*"Not fucking funny."*

The next night, I found myself having yet another evening in Raina's company. This time she suggested that I take her for a walk of the grounds and when I hesitated, she expressed her fears of leaving the house so soon after the attack. I felt my hand being forced. However, I conceded anyway, as at the very least I wouldn't have too long to wait to get back to Emmeline.

"You have a beautiful home," she told me, making me inwardly wince, and I had to admit to the same statement not holding even half as much weight as it did when Emmeline had said it.

"Thank you," I forced out.

"Have you lived here long?" she asked in an attempt at getting to know more about me, when in truth, I nearly just handed over Emmeline's book and told her to read that instead. But then, I also knew I was being unfair. In all honestly, I wished I could have just read her mind, but strangely, like my Siren, her mind was silent to me. It was just another thing that irked me.

"In 1865, my King once purchased this 33-acre plot under a different name from the Bolmer estate. That same year he commissioned an architect, John Davis Hatch, to build a 99-room mansion called Greystone," I told her, knowing that she came here knowing of my world, and the reason for this was down to her dreams, just as it was in Emmeline's case.

"What happened to it?"

"It was a home hardly used, so he thought the investment better served by building other homes along the Hudson," I told her, making her grin.

"So, you invested?" she stated with a knowing grin, that wasn't unpleasant and in fact, quite pretty. Not that I enjoyed admitting that to myself or the way my Demon readily agreed.

"I did indeed and had this country home built." I nodded back to the 15,000 square foot mansion I'd had built as an escape from the city should ever I need one. But as I looked back to see what she saw now, I noticed it was without its shine, for her eyes didn't hold the same wonder that Emmeline's had.

Of course, there was no doubt that Raina was a beautiful woman but there was none of the cuteness that I adored or that playful mirth dancing behind a pair of chocolate brown eyes. There were no curves I just wanted to press my fingertips into or a riot of soft bouncy curls I wanted to play with. And as far as I could tell, the woman had barely even the hint of a sense of humour to speak of.

*Not like my funny girl.*

Yet there was still something about her that made my

Demon respond and as much as I hated it, I knew it wasn't something I could overlook.

"Shall we walk this way," I suggested when a comfortable silence hung between us. I motioned towards the side of the house and over to where a glass roof covered an indoor swimming pool. But I soon realized my mistake as I was offering Raina a hand down the steps onto the gardens that surrounded it, feeling now a pair of eyes on us. I turned and my breath caught in my throat, as there was Emmeline, standing on the balcony to the room we now shared.

The moment our eyes met, she looked as though she had been caught doing something naughty, as if she was spying on us when I knew she hadn't been. I swear my heart ached as she tried to act natural. She even started to wave but then stopped herself before shaking her head and going back inside. I could see her mumbling to herself from here and Gods, but those curls I wanted to tame with my fist once more.

"Emmeline, isn't it?" Raina asked, making me swallow what felt like fucking acid at just hearing her say her name. I would have growled had my Demon let me.

*"It is,"* I forced out, making my body move as she had long ago gone out of sight, and standing here just waiting for more was pointless.

"I didn't realize she lived here with you," she said, making me reply honestly.

"I wouldn't have her living anywhere else." She looked shocked by this statement but obviously chose not to question it.

A short time later and after looking back towards that

balcony more times than I could count, I made my excuses
and ended our date early. I walked her back inside and told
her I had business to attend to, something she told me she
understood. She'd said she knew what a busy man I must be
having such an aspiring empire. I didn't know why, but the
comment didn't sit right with me, as she was always pointing
out the luxury in which I lived in, wanting me to express its
worth. Yet Emmeline rarely ever mentioned it.

In fact, it took me back to yesterday's conversation, one
that had pissed me off at the time. It was when Emmeline
had asked me about what would happen to her should the
unthinkable occur. How she wanted none of my money, just
that shithole apartment back and a car that barely fucking ran
and had no fucking heating. A fact I had growled at once
when she spoke about it.

Gods, but I still remembered the pain at seeing that box
of tins in the back of her car. It got to me every time,
knowing she had lived so frugally like that. Because I
wanted to give her everything. I wanted to dress her up in the
finest silks, adorn her skin with the most exquisite jewellery
and have her wrapped up in the softest sheets money could
buy. I wanted her to try food from around the globe,
prepared by the very best chefs, and drown her in a luxury
she never asked for.

*I wanted only the best for my Siren.*

Speaking of which, as soon as I escorted Raina to her
room, hoping she would get the hint in staying there, I went
straight to where I knew Emmeline would be. I was ashamed
to say, but when she wasn't with me, I kept her room locked,
still not trusting her not to try and run from me.

She was after all, still my prisoner.

It was only my brother that was permitted to unlock her door, which was why I was curious to find it open.

But more than that…

*She was gone.*

# CHAPTER II
# SWIMMINGLY GOOD IDEAS
## EMMELINE

I paced the floor and ignored Roger, who hissed at me after getting fed up with this. Gods, I was even making my damn cat feel uneasy. Not that this was hard to achieve, as watching me eating an orange could have the same effect. Man, did that cat hate oranges, just the sight of them and it went batshit crazy. I dropped one on the floor once when it rolled from my shopping bag. Jesus, but you would have thought I'd dropped some sort of kitty grenade. It did that mental flip out that cats sometimes do that leaves owners standing there asking what the hell just happened. I swear, he even did a back flip off the wall and somehow ended up at the back of the couch!

Well, as long as it kept its claws from me, then it could do whatever it damn well pleased. Although, I must have really pushed him over the edge as he got up, stretched and sashayed towards the balcony doors, granting me one of the short list of communications it had with me. These ran in the order of…

Feed me, bitch.

Let me out, bitch.

Or the one I really watched out for... *Get away from me, bitch*. This one was relatively low on my wary radar right now, being that the little shit wanted to go out.

"There you go, go crazy in your shit pit," I said with a chuckle. I had put its kitty litter out there as the weather was dry. Both myself and Kaiden had agreed that it was unwise to let him have free rein outside just yet. I still wasn't convinced about him not creating an uprising against humanity should he be able to recruit enough wildlife.

"Oh come, just do your business already," I said, thinking it best to wait for him and noticing the glass roof below that showed the indoor pool. One I had been desperate to go in since I got here, knowing it was one luxury I'd missed out on after my gym membership had run out. Swimming was about as energetic as I got, despite not liking to be out of my depth. But if I could put my feet down, then I would swim like a fish.

"Look, let me make this easier for you. You are going to turn around three times to the right and then realise this isn't doing it for you, so you do the same thing to the left. Then you will scratch your back legs, make a mess and then do your kitty shitting squat. Then you're gonna hiss at me when you're done and make more of a mess in retaliation, 'cause clearly, having a human slave to feed you and clean up after you isn't enough to endear me to you," I said, talking to Roger as I usually did when I was alone.

Yep, I was that sad.

Sad enough to know my cat's crapping routine down to a

tee, as he did the exact thing I said he would. Then he swayed his little furry ass back inside and just as I was sighing, muttering about how I should have held out for that rabbit, I noticed two figures walking into view below.

*"Gods, no,"* I whispered painfully the moment I saw them. Kaiden was playing the gentleman, once again, and offering Raina a hand down the steps that led onto the manicured lawn. But then as he did this, he must have felt my presence because he stopped and turned to face me. As for me, well I didn't know what to do. I didn't know whether to openly acknowledge them or pretend as if I hadn't. Or should I just stand and stare like a weirdo, something I was doing right now. So stupidly, I raised a hand to wave, stopping myself halfway.

*"Gods, Emme, just act cool for once, will you,"* I scolded, before turning around quickly and walking back into the room, now muttering to myself,

"Idiot, Emmeline… you looked like a foolish puppy dog just staring like… Whoa!" I shouted as I bumped into a large body, despite it not being as tall as Kaiden, it was still much bigger than I was in my stocking feet.

"A very cute puppy dog," Hel commented with a smirk, making me sigh. Then I blurted out,

"Do you think he really likes her?" At this he lost his smirk and released a sigh himself.

"Wait, don't answer that," I said, holding up a hand and walking past him, getting hissed at by Roger.

"Oh, who asked you!" I snapped, making Hel chuckle.

"Nice to see it hates everyone, not just me," he commented.

"It doesn't hate your brother," I pointed out, as surprisingly he even let Kaiden stroke him and purred whenever he did. I didn't even know the bloody thing knew how to sodding purr!

"It perhaps recognizes one of its own," he replied dryly, making me laugh at this and point out the obvious,

"You're also a Wrath Demon, Hel." His smirk was his reply to this before his words followed... that and a wink, as he said,

"Yeah, but I'm a lover not a fighter."

"Now I know that's bullshit," I laughed, calling him out.

"Damn, but I can't get anything by you... know me like a book, doll face." I faked a laugh and pointed at him.

"Ha, ha, good one."

"I do try, Emme," he answered, using my nickname, something that Kaiden wouldn't yet do.

"So, is that what you're doing here then... trying?" I questioned, making him grin.

"I might be here on my brother's behalf."

"Yeah, and what were your orders this time?" I asked with a sigh.

"To check for voodoo dolls and any pins in my brother's balls," he replied, making me throw my head back and laugh, as damn, he was funny.

"No voodoo dolls, but I might have given Roger a nail file to sharpen his claws on." He chuckled at this.

"I thought you said he liked him."

"What can I say, I still live in hope," I replied, making him wink at me and say,

"There's that spunky girl who broke into my club." I scoffed before looking towards the balcony once more.

"Were you really sent here by Kaiden?" I asked, making him shrug his shoulders.

"Truth be told, I wanted to check on you myself. I know all of this can't be easy, Emmeline." I released a sigh, both touched he felt this way and disappointed that Kaiden hadn't been the one to send him here.

"But I get why you're doing this and if it means anything, I admire you for it," Hel added, surprising me.

"You do?"

"Up until you came along, I believed I was the only one who cared with that amount of depth about my brother and now… well, there is you, and by doing this, I know you hold the same love for him as I do," Hel admitted freely, and why wouldn't he? They were as close as brothers ever could be.

"The same?" I teased.

"Well, I don't want you to turn him pussy whipped, obviously," was Hel's response to that and naturally, I laughed.

*"Like anyone could,"* I muttered, scoffing to myself.

"Oh, trust me, this is a side of my brother I have never seen before and nor did I think I ever would," he admitted, making my heart beat a little faster. "You have completely turned his world upside down and now, well let's just say, he would never want to see it straight again," he told me, and I let my hope bloom before squashing it down again with my own lack of self-confidence.

"You're just saying these things to cheer me up."

"Yeah, and ask yourself why I would even bother, you're not my Siren," Hel pointed out, making me stop and question why.

"Then why?"

"Because you're my brother's Siren and there is no one in this world or the next, I care about more. You mean something to him and that means you mean something to me, it's that simple," he stated with a shrug of his shoulders.

"Yeah, but what if I am not his Siren?" I asked, forcing the painful question out.

"Do you love him?" he surprised me by asking.

"Yes, more than anything," I answered honestly, because I did and knew this down to my very soul.

"Then only a Siren would love someone and still be prepared to sacrifice their love and happiness for the love and happiness of their Fated." I released a sigh at this, deflating back into one of the chairs.

"That's not true, many people in love would do the same thing. My Nanna used to say, that if you love something, let it go, if it comes back to you, then it's yours to keep, if not, then it was never yours in the first place." At this he released his own sigh and asked me,

"And what about you, Emmeline?"

"What about me?"

"You already let him go once and he came back to you, so when are you going to live by your own rule and stop trying to run from what is obviously yours to love?" His question had the power to pierce my heart, just like he knew it would, I could see it in his beautiful blue eyes.

"Gods, but you're annoyingly wise... do you know that?" I said as a way to ease the tension of such a serious conversation. He smirked, shrugged his shoulders which was a habit of his, and said,

"I have been known to 'out wise' even the wisest from time to time."

"Okay, you just ruined it." He laughed and said,

"Yeah, that didn't work, did it?" I shook my head, giggling.

"No but you can make it up to me, oh wise one." At this he raised a brow in question.

"And how would you propose I do that?" I grinned big and told him,

"You can take me swimming."

⚘

Ten minutes later, I was dipping my toe in the water, making Hel chuckle. This was seconds after I had pulled off my towel, making him wolf whistle at the sexiest bikini I owned. It was cobalt blue and was a wraparound style. It was also one that had a strap tied around my neck and two others that were adjustable at my back like a crop top. The front part that covered my breasts crossed over and wrapped around my waist, tying at my back in a floppy bow.

As for the bottoms, these were wide briefs with the sides cut out and replaced by three thin straps that sat snuggly over my hips. Of course, I had picked it with only one man in mind, and it wasn't the one making me blush right now. I was actually cursing the fact that I had never bought the one with the strappy triangles that barely covered my breasts and had a thong bottom when I had the chance, not being brave enough to wear it on holiday with Nat.

"I don't think that constitutes as swimming, doll face." I shot him a look over my shoulder before pulling the elastic from around my wrist and using it to tie up my hair high on my head, leaving some curls down on purpose. Then I stepped down into the water that, admittedly, was the perfect temperature.

The room was long, with a rectangular pool that had a row of mosaic tiled pillars, each depicting tasteful blue flowers which matched the centre of the pool. Plush seating and striped blue and cream loungers were positioned on one side, and the other was a wall of glass. These large glass panels also matched the ones on the roof that I could see from my balcony. It showed the beautiful grounds beyond, making me wonder if they opened somehow for those hot summer days.

As for now, the sun was setting, and I knew it would be dark soon. No doubt why, when we walked in here, Hel had turned the lights on. These were recessed along the one wall that wasn't glass and sat behind a coving up by the ceiling. One that I knew would offer a warm glow at night as it would reflect off the glass.

"You know the rest of the pool is just as warm," Hel stated, as he noticed that I was only swimming lengths to halfway before turning back.

"I don't like swimming out of my depth," I told him.

"But why, as you clearly know how to swim?" he asked, making me tell him,

"I almost drowned as a kid. Ever since then, I just kind of panic and go back to that day," I told him, making him look thoughtful for a moment. As though this was just another thing he deemed important enough to file away in that cunning mind of his.

After this, I continued to do lengths for another five minutes, concentrating solely on my strokes, before I realised it was no longer just me and Hel in the room.

We had been joined by another...

*Wrath Demon.*

# CHAPTER 12
# SWIMMING IN FEAR
## WRATH

The moment I realized she was gone, I tore through the house like a fucking mad man! I had my phone in my hand calling Franklin, knowing his eyes would be glued to all the security screens like I paid him to fucking do!

*"Where is she?!"* I all but roared down the phone in my near blind rage. Had she tried to leave because of what she had seen when I was walking with Raina? Had the sight upset her enough that she had somehow figured how to pick the fucking lock? Fuck, but I was near insanity! That was until he said,

"She is swimming, my Lord Wrath."

"Swimming?!" I snapped.

"Hel is watching over her," he added, making me growl before issuing one last order,

"Turn off the screen for I will deal with this!" Then I cut the call just as he was replying, not doubt with the usual, my Lord Wrath crap I had no fucking time for!

Fuck, but what had Hel been thinking?!

I ran to the pool, near fucking skidding around the corner in my haste, making my brother snigger when I came to a blinding halt the second I saw her.

*"Gods!"* I hissed, getting rock hard in seconds. It felt as if all the blood from my head had just rushed straight to my dick! Then I walked slowly towards my brother, unable to take my eyes off the way her curvy little body glided through the water. Doing so as if she had been born to swim in it. Of course, water and Sirens were a myth, just like the tales of them luring sailors to their deaths from beneath the water's surface. No, their beauty could have power enough to do that, for I felt like fucking drowning myself just so I could stay under the water long enough to see the rest of her.

"What... why...?" Okay, yeah, so this was all I managed to get out, making my brother chuckle again.

"I swear I tried not to look," he told me, making me growl,

"Had those eyes belonged to anyone other than my brother, I would have fucking ripped them out." He outright laughed at this.

"Hence why I told Franklin where she would be, who would be with her and to turn off the fucking screen," Hel replied, making me scoff a laugh this time, as I had done the same thing, only my brother had the power of foresight.

"Then I am thankful," I told him.

"But answer me this, why is she only swimming halfway?"

"Ah, well that is quite a story," Hel replied, having me intrigued.

"How so?"

"She nearly drowned as a kid." I hissed a breath.

"Fuck! Is she safe? It looks like she knows how to swim but…"

"Calm, brother, she can swim just fine. No, she told me that if she is out of her depth then fear takes hold and the ability to swim is lost to that fear," he replied, stopping me with a hand to my chest as I swear, I had been about to dive in there and save her from… well, herself.

"I see," I said more calmly this time.

"I know that look," he commented when I did indeed wonder how she would fare once out of her depth, only with her in my arms… would she cling on tight like I hoped she would?

"I am tapping you out," I said, referring to the times mine and my brother's style of fighting turned into wrestling on the mats. The bastard loved to find new ways to take me down.

"Yeah, I thought you would say that," he said on a chuckle slapping me on the back.

"Go and enjoy your Siren's fears." I had to smirk at that, one that turned into a full grin when she finally noticed that another Demon had arrived.

*Her Demon Wrath.*

## CHAPTER 13
# OUT OF MY DEPTH
### EMMELINE

The moment I saw him, I stopped swimming. I quickly let my feet find the bottom of the pool, keeping my body hidden as if I had done something wrong. Because really, there wasn't that much difference between sexy underwear sets and bikinis.

Was I playing with fire again?

Something Kaiden had often accused me of doing. Well, from the look of the burning gaze in his darkening green eyes, I would say so. I watched as Hel slapped his brother on the back, said something with a chuckle and then walked out, leaving me alone with his brother. With a Demon that looked as though he wanted to…

*Devour me whole.*

Then, without saying a word, he removed his jacket, tossing it casually to one of the sun loungers that also held my towel. One I was suddenly desperate to get to.

*"Take down your hair!"* he suddenly ordered, and I swear the sound of his stern voice did crazy things to my

core. Was it possible for lady bits to flutter? Well, if it was, I think mine just took off like a damn hummingbird!

Of course, when I was too stunned to do as he commanded, he raised an expectant brow at me.

"This will go easier on you if you obey me," he told me, making me swallow hard, and that hummingbird flutter, flipped me the finger and told me it was out of here! At this I opened my mouth and then closed it again. A sight that obviously amused him, as he smirked to himself looking to the floor and granting me that delicious sight of his perfect jawline. He had recently shaved the sides of his head, getting rid of the week's growth, and I swear it made him look even more formidable, if such a thing were possible.

Of course, my eyes suddenly forgot all about his brutally handsome face at the sight of the body now coming on show. As, with a mouth-watering twist of his body, he pulled off his light-grey T-shirt, making me unable to hold back my response as I uttered a breathless,

*"Oh Gods, help me."* Again, his smirk deepened at this, obviously hearing it for himself. I knew this for certain the moment he told me,

"There isn't a God out there that could help you now, *for no one could keep you from me,"* he said, adding to this heart pounding threat by tugging open his heavy belt and dragging it slowly through the loops.

"I...I... think I should..."

"Do as I command? I agree." He finished yanking the end of the leather through the last loop of his jeans before making a show of dragging it through his large hands.

"W-what are you... going to do with that?" I asked after first clearing my throat.

"That depends on you and what you do for me," he told me, making me jump when he snapped it in his hands and the slap of leather echoed in the large room. I quickly reached up and took down my hair, doing so quickly enough that I was fumbling with shaky fingers.

Again, *he enjoyed the sight.*

Then, once my hair was down, he made a show of dropping the belt and I felt as if I could finally breathe again. This, despite half of me, the darker half, wondering what would have happened had I not done as he asked? Would he have used it on me, spanked my ass with it or just simply used it to tie me up? Gods, but I had to stop myself from tying my hair back up again to find out.

Just the sight of that powerful, painted torso on show with line after line of muscle had me almost fearful of what he could do to me. He was incredible and looked indestructible. Like nothing could beat him, nothing could even touch him. And he knew it. That confidence was so hot, it made me feel like some willing victim of his. Even just the way he yanked his jeans open, well, it stole my breath in a shameful whoosh of expelled air. Of course, the moment I saw he wasn't wearing anything beneath, I quickly turned around and mouthed,

*'Oh God,'* jumping the moment I heard him enter the water and spinning around to face the devil at my back.

"This is a bad idea," I told him, making him grin, and I swear it was all his Demon this time. Bloody hell, but just the way he glided through the water as he walked closer with most of his body still on show, seeing as we were in the shallow end and he was so tall. So much taller than me. He had the ability to make me feel tiny, because every inch of him was so big. Speaking of which, I forced myself not to look at the most obvious naked place my eyes wanted to travel to.

"This was your idea," he told me, making me shake my head a little.

"What? Did you really think you could sneak down here wearing that and I wouldn't find out, that I wouldn't crave to drink in the sight for myself?" he asked, making me gulp.

"I didn't think…"

"Oh, I think you knew exactly what you were doing," he interrupted, and suddenly I was so nervous I felt myself realising he was right. I had worn my sexiest swimwear, hoping for this very reason. Again, I just couldn't seem to help myself. I couldn't seem to stop craving his attention, despite knowing how wrong it was. Which was why the next emotion to flood me was regret.

"I shouldn't be here," I admitted, making him growl,

"Yet here you are."

"I just wanted a swim," I told him weakly, making him tut with his tongue hitting the roof of his mouth at the sound of my weak excuses.

"That's not all you wanted," he said confidently and again, why was I so attracted to and not turned off by his arrogance? Was it because I knew he had the power to back it up? Did that give him the right? I had no clue, I only knew how it made me feel and right now, I needed to get away from these feelings he ignited.

*I need to run from my need.*

"I am just going to…" I started to say as I made my escape, walking past him and trying to give him a wide berth so I was out of his grasp. However, I had only managed three steps through the water before a dark barrier appeared suddenly, making me cry out.

*"You're going nowhere, my little temptation,"* he said in a dark tone after his wing had created a wall in front of me. I sucked back a startled gasp at just the sight of it. They were huge, leaving me gaping up at them seeing that they were at least seven feet tall in height. They curled up at the top, spiked with the same horns that appeared on Kaiden when he was every inch of Wrath. Large bones the width of his arm, rose up and bent with knee joints to form the zigzag shape as they connected first to his back. Then they rose up to a point, tipped with a huge, hooked black claw, one that shone under the light that reflected from the glass. From this main wing bone, attached were other finger-like bones, long and thinner, that curved down, disappearing under the water. In between these black skin-covered bones were interlocking scales of thick leathery skin. Each tipped with deadly, sharp points that I knew would lie flat when he was relaxed or flying, but would also fan out when he needed the lethal touch, creating a wall of spikes. Thankfully for me, they were currently relaxed and looked smooth, appearing slightly less threatening.

But like I said, they were huge, and with him standing in the middle, this meant that they both reached the sides of the pool, acting as a barricade to stop me reaching the shallower end. But then, as I tried to reach the side, I found his wing coming towards me and unless I was to go out of my depth, I had no choice but to go the way he wanted me. I was being herded inwards as they started to close in around me, making me yelp. Then, before I could get away, he pulled them both in together, and I had nowhere else to go but closer to the man in the middle.

"Okay, okay! Just stop it now... Kaiden!" I shouted, making him chuckle as they funnelled me closer, pushing my back so I had no choice but to swim into him. This brought me in close enough this time that he reached out and framed my waist with his large hands. He hadn't even needed to take a single step towards me to get what he wanted. No, he had used his wings to simply collect up his prize.

"There now, that's better," he stated, squeezing my flesh and making me feel the bite of his fingers in silent reprimand for making him wait. After this he made his wings disappear, and that darkness that had cast eerie shadows over the water was suddenly gone.

"You need to let me go," I told him, trying to pull myself free of his hold, making him growl down at me before he started walking forward.

"Wait, what are you doing?!" I shouted in panic as the closer he travelled to the other side, the less traction my feet made on the bottom.

"I am taking you out of your depth," he stated brazenly, making me gasp.

"But I can't swim out of my depth!" I shrieked, making him grin before telling me in a knowing tone,

"Then you will just have to hold on tight, won't you?" After this he took that last step that made my toes lose the last of the floor before I had no choice but to quickly wrap my arms around his neck.

"Kaiden, no! I don't..."

"Hey, look at me now." I did as I was told thanks to his stern, commanding tone.

"Do you think that I would I ever let anything happen to you?" he asked, making me shake my head telling him no. However, the moment he let my waist go, I cried out his name,

"Kaiden!" He chuckled as he'd only let me go long enough so he could band a strong arm around my back, holding me more securely but yet giving him the freedom of one hand. Then he continued to walk, being that the water was only up to the top of his eight pack.

"Okay, okay, that's close enough, you can stop walking now," I said, and his response was a cocky one.

"Oh, I don't know, I think you can hold me a little tighter than that." Then he took another step until the water came to his chest and I freaked, pulling myself up him and wrapping my legs around his waist, with my feet crossed over his firm bare ass.

"There we go," he replied arrogantly, making me growl at him in response.

"And there's my kitten's growl," he teased playfully, grinning as if he was having the most fun ever.

"I would threaten to bite you but that would just spur you on!" I snapped, making him laugh and he put a hand to his neck where my mark was still on show and not yet healed.

"Are you ever going to let it heal?" I asked as it still looked as fresh as when I first did it. Even on a human it would have looked better by now. Which was when he shocked me.

"The longer I leave it fresh, the deeper the scar will hold."

"You're not kidding?" I asked, making him give me a pointed look.

"I told you, I wanted your mark forever on my skin," he stated as if this was evident.

"But seriously, you want it to actually scar?" I asked again, too shocked to believe it was true and that he hadn't just been teasing me like I thought he might.

"You know me well enough, Emmeline, what do you think? Do I ever say things that don't hold weight of truth?" he asked, and I let it slip...

"Only when you're promising to let me go." At this he squeezed me tighter.

"Indeed, and a necessary lie at the time that I am not ashamed of admitting." I sighed at this.

"Then how do I know that you won't continue to lie to get what you want?" I tested.

"You don't, just like I won't yet believe that you will not run from me... so you see, we are at a crossroads with neither of us walking the road of trust," he said, and I had realised he had reached even closer to the other side, being tall enough that he kept our shoulders and heads out of the water.

"That's not a great foundation for a relationship," I pointed out, making him grin.

"A foundation you yourself laid, little Halo, for you grew the seed of mistrust and watered it all by yourself." I huffed at this, despite his amusement.

"Can you really blame me, I thought you would kill me?" I reminded him, making him squeeze me tighter at just the idea of hurting me.

"Insanity and the loss of my mind wouldn't have been able to make me hurt you, let alone take you from me."

"You did bite me," I pointed out.

"Yes, and I will continue to do so… *now that I know you like it.*" He added this on a Demonic purr.

"And who said…" I stopped the moment he raised a brow at me.

"Really? You want to play that game with me? For I would be more than happy to test the theory, as you may be in water, but even that won't be enough to hide your *wet arousal from me.*" I shuddered at this, especially when he said this last part by purposely rubbing his erection against me. Then he started to lower his lips to my neck, opening his mouth and taking in my flesh, getting ready to bite down and making me shout out,

"Okay, I like it!" His bite quickly turned into a grin against my skin. Then he pulled back and with his free hand, he skimmed the tops of my breasts that admittedly were pushed together and held higher thanks to the awesome support of my bikini.

"Just as I like these," he said, tracing the line of blue material that covered only half of my breasts, making me want to beg him to tug on the bow at my back that was a single action away from releasing them. A single flick of his wrist was all it would have taken but instead, his hand travelled not to my back but down my centre, teasing his fingertips down the line of my cleavage. Then he kept going, teasing me until he leaned back enough so he could get his hand down between us and see for himself the erotic journey he was on. But then I started to lose my hold on him, and I panicked. I pressed myself against him, slamming my breasts against his chest, making him chuckle.

His hand went to my hip, tugging his fingers in the three straps there, as if I was some instrument he was playing.

"So delicious. Gods, woman, but you make my fucking mouth water," he told me, making me bury my head into his neck so he wouldn't see how happy that compliment made me. Because it was wrong to want this, to want the attention I was addicted to. But then I had noticed the way he had started making his way to a shallower part, so my heaving chest was out of the water completely. Then my back touched the side of the pool, and I shrieked out at the cool tile on my skin. But my cries of resistance ended quickly as he put an arm under my ass and hoisted me further up his hard body. Then he dipped his head enough so he could take one creamy breast into his mouth. This made my head fall back as I cried out for a very different reason this time. He started biting over where my cold nipple was straining against the material, rolling it through his teeth and making me shudder as the beautiful pain shot straight to my clit.

I could feel his cock against me, seeing that my bikini bottoms were barely a barrier between us, and he was but one thrust away from claiming me like he wanted... *like we both wanted.*

"Be mine!" he growled, making me shake my head as my lips wouldn't let me speak and deny him. He snarled before going back to my delicious torture. I cried out even louder at this and a single second after his hardest bite yet, he let go and demanded more firmly this time,

"Give yourself to me, do it now, Emmeline!" At that I barely had it in me to shake my head, forcing the action and making him suddenly fist a hand in my wet hair.

*"You will be ours!"* His Demon spoke before he claimed the only piece of me I would allow, taking everything I could give him in a kiss. I cried out, something he swallowed up as

he plundered my mouth, tasting every inch of me with his tongue. Now duelling with mine in a fight for dominance I would never have a chance at winning.

But then his hand started to tug dangerously at the straps at my hip, and I knew he was seconds away from taking what he wanted, regardless of my wishes. Because deep down he knew how much I wanted this, how much I wanted him. Which was why we both knew it would never really be taking me by force. He would never have it in him to do that, he had honour and respect and was a real man in every sense of the good word.

"Kaiden, please," I pleaded as he tore his lips from mine and buried his head in my neck, taking my flesh in his mouth. I knew how he wanted to claim me. That we were seconds away from crossing that line. The one that in his mind, would make me his forever. The bite of my flesh at the same time taking the very last barrier between us, as he drank down my blood, thrusting up inside me. Which was why I caressed the top of his wet hair back, letting my hand slip down to the back of his neck and what I knew to be soft spot for him.

*"Please... not like this, honey,"* I told him in a tender tone, making him let go of my flesh instantly as his hands relaxed at my hips.

"Fuck, but I have never wanted anything so badly, never fucking craved a single thing until there was you," he told me, forcing himself to stop, and I squeezed his neck in response. Because my words would have been too dangerous at that moment. To admit that I felt the same way would be all he needed to take that as a green light to go. To give us both what we wanted.

What we both desired.

*What we needed.*

But then I knew I would never forgive myself for denying him the chance at his fate. One that could have been Raina, as much as it felt like it could also be me. I had to be sure. It had to be an absolute. Because I would always wonder. I would always doubt. I would let it fester and grow like poison. Because I couldn't just eradicate six years of dreaming of them together. Not without his certainty, and despite how right being in his hold now felt, I couldn't help but worry that had Raina been the one to come along first, that it would be her here in his arms now.

And I was terrified.

Terrified that I had…

*Fucked with Fate.*

## CHAPTER 14
# SECONDS

After this, he walked me back into my safe depth and I reluctantly let my legs uncurl from around his waist. Because he didn't need to say it, but I knew it was time for us to let go of temptation by getting out of the pool. So, to ease the tension, I walked towards the steps and before I could stop myself, I quickly turned and threw both my hands forward. I ended up pushing a fair amount of water at him, splashing him in the face and soaking him. His face, however, was a complete picture of cool, easily hiding his shock and disbelief. He simply scrubbed a hand down his wet face, pushing the drips from his skin as he closed his eyes, keeping his features composed.

I couldn't help but snigger, a song that died the moment he opened his eyes, and his Demon was looking back at me through darkness, as all the green was long gone.

"Right," he said seriously, and that's when I held up my hands and started walking backwards.

"Hey now, I was just playing." At this his eyes started to glow before he grinned mischievously and then said,

"Yeah, I know and now… *it's my turn.*" This was my only warning as he held out his hands and suddenly the water started to pull back from in front of me as if it was being sucked out by some kind of current. Then, before I could question it further, I realised he had gathered it up behind me, making it suddenly come crashing into my back. I naturally fell forward into his arms as the water splashed up around us, making my hair practically cover my face. I spluttered the water from my lips and suddenly burst out laughing at how funny his come-back was. I felt his hands pushing all my hair back and found Kaiden's warm green eyes looking down at me once more, as he was back to grinning.

"You win, Demon," I said, making him chuckle, before suddenly I was thrown over his shoulder, crying out. However, he lifted me higher with no effort at all, keeping my head out of the water, until it was shallow enough to rest me over his large muscles.

"Of course, I did," he replied in a cocky tone before I started complaining.

"Put me down, you big brute!" I stilled when he smacked my ass playfully, one that was practically bare thanks to my bikini bottom that had ridden up.

"Quiet, woman of mine!" he growled in a teasing tone, and I when I started kicking out, he turned his head and actually bit my bum, making me shriek!

"Mmm, like a juicy peach," he said, chuckling to himself and in turn, I decided to get him back by smacking his own ass, one my head was quite close to.

"Two can play at that game!" I shouted, smacking it again and making him roar with laughter.

"Play all you want, I like it... like a gentle caress," he mocked as his naked body took the steps out of the water and I swear, had I been lower down, then I would have bitten him back, as his ass was certainly yummy. However, my ass was ripe for the taking, being practically level with his face, as all he had to do was turn his head and my bouncing cheek was right there.

"This fucking ass! Gods, woman, what I want to do to you and it!" he snarled into my cheek before biting it again and making me shout,

"Don't leave marks there too!" When really, I so badly wanted him to, knowing I would get a sick high off seeing his marks all over my body.

But before I could complain some more, he stroked a gentle palm down my ass where he had just bitten before gripping my cheek in his hand. I moaned as he used this hold to lower me back to my feet, bending so he didn't lose contact with my ass.

"You can let go now," I said, as he still had it in his firm hold.

"You know, I don't think I can," he teased, making me swat at his arm before stepping away from him. Of course, I couldn't keep up with acting annoyed as I burst into a fit of giggles, loving how playful he could be with me. He gently brushed back some of my hair with his fingers, and looked down at me as though I was the most endearing creature he had ever seen. Then, I shivered, something he must have taken was for another reason, as he reached for my towel, before wrapping it around me and tugging the ends back towards him.

"There, all wrapped up like a gift," he said with a grin, and before I could reply, he kissed me. This time it was soft and gentle, making me unable to hold myself back from melting into him. He pulled back after a minute of tender kissing and proceeded to rub my arms, trying to help me get warm and dry.

"What about you?" I asked shyly, making him let me go and hold his arms out to the sides, and I swear I could have licked the drips off his massive biceps. Gods, but I loved his arms. And his chest. Oh, and his rippling eight pack. But then I loved his back too. And those muscles on his sides that looked like grills. Okay, so it was safe to say I loved the sight of all of him.

But I used my own towel to wrap around his waist to cover up his very obvious erection, making him laugh.

"There we go, temptation hidden," I stated with my own smirk.

*"No, it fucking isn't!"* he growled, looking me up and down as if he wanted to eat me up. So, I quickly snagged his T-shirt and tugged it on. It look like a tent on me.

"There, the girls are safely covered," I said, and he grinned.

"If you think that makes you safe from me, then you forget my claw too soon," he said, making a point of allowing a single finger to turn, using it to draw me closer, curling it inwards. I gulped at the sight of it, knowing it could cut through steel, granting him an even greater depth of danger. So, I thought it wise to do as I was told, making me take a step closer to him, holding deathly still as he used the back of it to caress down my cheek.

"Gods, but you are so beautiful, you make my heart ache, girl," he told me, making me suck in a quick breath and just as he leaned down to kiss me, a sound behind interrupted us.

"Oh, I am sorry! I didn't know anyone was here, I was just going for a swim." I gasped, pulled back and stepped away from Kaiden, making him rumble his displeasure down at me. However, the moment I caught sight of the true beauty in front of me, I couldn't help but take the hit to my confidence, despite what Kaiden had said seconds ago.

She looked like a water goddess, wearing a pure-white one-piece that was only called that as a thin strip of material joint the top to the bottom. Small pieces of her bikini covered her nipples but left little else to the imagination as it went down into a Y shape, joining barely-there briefs. A see-through kaftan offered no protection from anything, as you could see all of her, and no doubt a light breeze would be enough to make it look as though she was smuggling a pair of gold nuggets in her top.

"Oh, it's fine, we just finished, I mean me... I just finished... erm, Kaiden, I am not sure, are you finished?" I asked in a flustered way as if we weren't together, and he narrowed his gaze at me before looking up and straight at Raina.

*"We have finished!"* he declared, doing so in a way I knew was him making a point of telling her we had been in here together, despite my bumbled attempt at claiming otherwise.

"Oh, okay, I guess I will swim alone," she replied, looking disappointed, but then to hide this she pulled her pointless kaftan off and tossed it to the side, showing now her swimsuit was hiding even less with the thong back.

Then she executed the perfect dive into the deep end, making me instantly jealous at her being capable of doing that. Her sleek body reminded me of a graceful mermaid, as though she had been born knowing how to swim. She rose to the surface and pushed all her golden hair back as if she was a Bond girl emerging from the ocean. But Kaiden wasn't watching her...

He was watching me, watch her.

"Come, Emmeline," he said in a hard tone, before taking my hand in his and walking me from the room, just as Raina's sing song voice said,

"I look forward to seeing you tomorrow night, Kai." I gritted my teeth at that but remained silent as I let myself be tugged along, feeling my lovely loved-up glow all but sucked out of me. I was so lost in my turmoil that I didn't realise I was even back in the room until I heard the door slam, making me jump. Then he left me standing there as he walked towards his bag of clothes, reaching inside and grabbing the first thing to hand. Then, ignoring me, he dressed quickly, letting me know he was angry.

*"What's wrong?"* I asked in a quiet voice, making him snap,

"What is fucking *right* with this fucked up deal of yours!?"

"But you agreed that it..." I tried to say, but he quickly interrupted me, making me realise this was most likely going to be a common theme to his argument.

"I made a mistake, one I knew it to be the second I

agreed to it, but it was what you wanted!" he argued back before I could finish.

"But, Kaiden…"

"Did you ever care to ask what I wanted!?" he threw back at me, making me flinch. He did up the new pair of jeans he had dragged up his legs in his anger.

"I knew what you wanted," I told him softly.

"Yes… *I wanted you!*" I sucked in a startled breath at this and repeated his fatal flaw in that statement.

*"Wanted?"* Past tense… not good.

"Don't twist my words, Emmeline, or you will get extra ones you will not like, nor do you want to fucking hear them!" he warned back in return.

"Maybe they are words I need to hear all the same," I stated, making him snarl,

"Not until this shit is done!" he barked back, making me flinch as if he had struck me. Then I watched as he dragged a black T-shirt over his head, covering his tensed muscles before storming to the door.

"Wait, where are you going?" I asked quickly,

"To give you what you want!" he snapped back before slamming the door behind him and for once in his rage, he forgot to lock it. But my mouth dropped open in shock, asking what he meant by that. Was he just giving me space or was it something far worse…?

*Was he going for a second swim?*

## CHAPTER 15
# SILENT HEARTBREAK

*More tears.*

I couldn't stand my tears.

But I couldn't stand not knowing even more. Which was why I got dressed quickly and walked out onto the balcony, so I could see for myself if he had returned to her.

*He hadn't.*

I swear the relief I felt should have been a crime. Because I should have been encouraging him to do just that. But honestly, I was emotionally exhausted. Constantly torn between what I wanted and what I knew was right. It was like my heart was being pulled one way and then the other, creating fucking whiplash!

Because the reality was that I was tired of trying to do the right thing. I was so done trying to be this good person when my own heart was breaking because of it. And not just because I was trying to fight with what I wanted but also because I was constantly fighting against what Kaiden wanted.

And what he wanted… *was me.*

I knew that now! Because he was right, I hadn't taken what he wanted into account, just how I felt. I had made his decision for him, backing him into a corner and forcing him to try and feel something for Raina when it was obvious there wasn't anything. Just because I had written her into Kaiden's life, it didn't mean she automatically held a place written there in his heart.

*Why couldn't I trust that?*

Why couldn't I trust his need, his want, his desires for me. Gods, but he had barely even looked at Raina nearly naked. But he had looked at me. Oh boy, had he looked.

I felt like a fucking fool! As if I was torturing him and why? Because I lacked the confidence in myself to feel like I was good enough for him. Because I couldn't trust that I was everything he could possibly want and need, when his words had told me so, over and over again.

I had to go and find him!

I had to go and tell him how I felt. How I wanted him for myself. How I was ready to put an end this all of this and let him claim me for himself. How I needed him as much as he needed me. Suddenly, I found myself running from the room and thinking of the only place he was likely to be, I made my way to his office, ready to burst in there and tell him everything. But then, the moment I turned a corner, I heard him roaring in anger, making me stop dead.

"Calm, brother, before you destroy the whole fucking room."

"I don't give a fucking shit about the room!" he bellowed back and the sound of something smashing against the door made me flinch back even further. Of course, I knew he

124

would never hurt me, but that didn't make his rage any less scary.

"I can't go on like this any longer!" Kaiden said after first panting through his rage.

"Yes, I can see that," Hel stated dryly, making his brother growl.

"I just want to claim her before..." he stopped suddenly, making me frown and brace myself, as I had a feeling I wasn't supposed to hear any of this. Any of what came next.

"Before what?" Kaiden must have given his brother a telling look as Hel soon added,

"Oh please don't tell me..."

"I can't help it, there is something about this Raina that I just can't deny, and it is a feeling I don't fucking want!" he snapped, and my hands flew to my mouth to cover the gasp of pain that wanted to escape.

He felt something for her.

*Felt something for Raina.*

Oh Gods, but what I done?! I felt the tears answer me, as I had done exactly what I had set out to do. I had given an Enforcer a chance at his Siren. A chance at living his destiny... I had given him back his fate.

"It's why you want to claim her so badly, you think that once you do, then these thoughts you have for Raina will go."

*"I know they will,"* Kaiden stated firmly, and it was honestly almost too much to bear. I started shaking my head, biting my lip until I tasted blood and physical pain was another hurt for me to feel, adding to my misery. *To my heartbreak.*

I had to get out of there!

I had to escape this torture, but then I knew I had nowhere to go. So, I did the only thing I could do. That was the only thing left in my power to do. I ran back to my room, wishing that locking it would have been enough to keep him out. To keep this pain away. So instead, I did the only thing I could, ignoring the way Roger hissed at me from his cushion. I ran myself a bath and tried to soak my pain away. But no matter how much I scrubbed at my skin, I could never rid myself the memory of his touch beneath, one that felt eternally imprinted there.

But then how could I be angry at Kaiden, when this had been all my own doing... *a misery of my very own making.*

I couldn't. Which was why, after I was assured that all my tears had run dry and I had no more of an excuse to hide in here, having washed all there was to wash, I got out. Then, after brushing my hair, towel drying the curls the best I could, I dressed in my comforting pjs and fluffy socks. After that, I walked back into the room, fully intent on curling up on the bed and continuing to wallow in my own self-pity. However, what I didn't expect was Kaiden sitting there on the edge, with a foot up against the frame and his elbow to his knee so his hand could prop up his head, cupped by a palm to his forehead.

He looked up at me and stated quickly,

"I left the door unlocked."

*"I know,"* I replied quietly.

"You didn't try and run." Again, this was said as a statement.

"No, *I didn't,"* I answered before biting my lip to stop it quivering. Gods, but it was so painful to look at him, knowing now what I knew of his mind... *how torn he was.*

He released a sigh at that before straightening his legs and standing, then walking closer to me. However, the step I took back made him pause. A frown appeared on his face, yet it wasn't enough to stop him from continuing in his footsteps for long, as he was soon towering above me.

*"My good girl,"* he whispered softly, now raising my face up so he could run the pad of his thumb under my eyes.

"I am sorry I was angry at you," he told me gently, making me close my eyes and swallow hard before nodding, knowing I didn't trust myself to speak. I was the only one however, as he made a pretty obvious guess.

"I made you cry?"

"It doesn't matter now," I replied, opening my sore, traitorous eyes, giving him all the evidence he needed to make this claim.

"It matters to me, for I should never be the cause for your tears," he told me, but before I could reply, he swept my legs from under me and picked me up so he could carry me to the bed. Then he lay me down and the moment he scanned the length of me, he smirked as he realised what I was wearing. My pyjama choice tonight had little pigs flying over clouds on the pants and a cropped top that showed a bit of my belly. The top had a bigger pig curled up asleep on a cloud, that said, 'Count Piggy Snorts Not Cows Snores'

*"Cute,"* he muttered to himself, making me blush before he tore the T-shirt off his head for the second time tonight. Then, as he got into bed next to me, I turned on my side, knowing that I couldn't face him. However, he didn't take this as a deterrent, as he simply wrapped an arm around me, and tucked me closer to him. Then he snaked an arm under my neck, so I was resting against his muscle. After this he

reached down and snagged the sheets and covered us both up, this time keeping his jeans on. Then he held me tight to him and whispered,

*"I am sorry I made you cry, Little Halo."*

I nodded a little, telling him a little how I felt but still knowing...

It wasn't enough to sleep through my...

*Silent heartbreak.*

## CHAPTER 16
# FANCY BALLS

After this, I knew things had to change.
*I had to change.*
Which was why I spent the next few days being standoffish with Kaiden, trying to allow him the time he needed without me making this harder for him. I had set us both down this journey, and now I just needed to be brave enough to discover what was waiting for me at our destination.

Of course, he knew something was wrong. Because well... he wasn't an idiot. Which meant that he didn't accept my excuses when I told him I felt too tired to go to the club or had a headache and that was my reason to sleep early. He knew I was lying.

He knew something had changed in me... *He just didn't know what.*

However, it was on the third night, with only two nights of our deal left to endure, that one Wrath brother had hit his limit. The one I didn't expect to find storming into my room after first unlocking the door.

"Right, get your ass up, we are getting you out of this room," Hel stated after striding his confident body inside, wearing one of his usual suits, this one being navy blue. A crisp white shirt was seen underneath his tailored jacket and was without a tie.

"And where are we going?" I asked with a sigh, putting my laptop off to one side after long ago finishing my work for the day. As well, I had done every item description I had been sent and for once was well before any deadlines. But then, I hadn't had much else to do, seeing as all my meals were brought to me each day, and keeping the room clean took me all of thirty seconds considering I only had to straighten the bed. My clothes seemed to magically wash themselves and fresh towels appeared out of nowhere. Of course, I knew that someone did all of this, but seeing that I would walk out of the bathroom and find a pile of freshy washed clothes and towels, then it was like a housekeeping fairy had been assigned to the room.

Not that I was even close to running out of clothes, as the walk-in wardrobe had been fully stocked. A wardrobe with not only my own clothes, but what looked like a whole shop, with everything in my size that had been bought for me. Which was why I was now wearing a soft grey sweater dress that had a big cowl neck, that kept falling off one shoulder. Of course, I also had to add a strappy black top underneath in case the wide neck fell forward, and everyone would get an eyeful of my black bra. To this I added a pair of black skinny jeans and tied half my hair up in an attempt to tame it back from my face.

"Anywhere away from these four walls," he said in answer to my question, looking around the room as if it was the prison cell it sometimes felt like. Because despite me not trying to run from the room when Kaiden had mistakenly left it unlocked, he had not risked it again. I think this was down to my cold treatment of him as he must have felt that I still hadn't forgiven him after our argument. If only he knew the truth.

That I had been ready to ask him to make me his. That I had been only seconds away from bursting inside his office and asking him to claim me once and for all. If only he knew it all.

"Do I need my jacket?" I asked, trying to find out if this outing was beyond the walls of this mansion.

"I think my brother would have my balls if I was to go that far, I only allowed you to go in the pool and he looked ready to tear my head off when finding you missing." I chuckled at this as I followed him out of the room.

"So, I realised that my brother never actually showed you around the place," Hel said as way of excuse for this moment of freedom.

"Well, technically, I am still a prisoner," I reminded him, making him smirk at me as we passed what looked like more bedrooms.

"There are eight guest rooms, with two suites, one belonging to myself on the opposite side of the house, with Kai's... well, I am sure you remember it."

"Haha," I commented, making him laugh. "You're enjoying this, aren't you?"

"Oh, trust me, doll face, when you're as old as we are, then you find joy in anything different. After so long, we are kind of hard to shock or surprise."

"So, I must have been like an early Christmas," I joked.

"Oh, sweetheart, you were all of my brother's Christmas' come at once." I couldn't help but smile at this.

"I've been a bit hard on him lately," I admitted feeling guilty. Although I had to confess that it was nice to have someone to talk to about it. Roger most definitely didn't count.

"Yeah, I gathered," he replied, making me wince.

"You did?"

"Not sure if you realised this yet, but my brother has a mean ass temper, always has done and well, it's what makes him one of the scariest motherfuckers in our world. He gives no mercy and takes no prisoners... curvy little curly blondes notwithstanding, of course." I laughed at this.

"Yeah, I kind of wrote a book about him, remember? Trust me, I get that he has a temper."

"Yes, but did you also know that these feelings he is experiencing are things he's never felt before. Finding one's humanity can be a bitch I am sure... looks fucking Heaven to me... What? We like Hell," he added when I gave him a confused look.

"I guess I haven't made it any easier," I confessed.

"Don't be too hard on yourself, Doll, I know you care, as does my brother." I raised a brow at him this time,

"He read the same book, remember?" he reminded me, making me blush whenever I thought of that fact.

"This here is the library," he said, opening a door and showing me the old-fashioned room that was floor to ceiling shelving filled with books. Also, an array of antique furniture was dotted around the room, offering comfortable, cosy places for you to enjoy a good book and relax. It also had large bay windows that flooded the room with natural light and had an inbuilt bench seat that wrapped around the semi-circle.

"Nice... spend much time in there do you?" I teased, making him reply,

"I have been known to enjoy a good book or two after beating the shit out of my enemies and sending them back to my father to play with." Then he winked at me when my mouth dropped in shock.

"You do not!" I slapped his arm, making him smirk down at me. Damn, but I knew I should have worn my boots and not just stuffed my feet into a pair of ballet flats. Even Hel made me feel like a short-arse.

"And you will never know," he said playfully. After this room, we continued on and as soon as I saw the next space, I started getting excited, jumping up and down and dragging him inside.

"Whoa, okay, so it's not just one type of pool you enjoy playing in then," he commented as I fawned over the black felted pool table that was utterly gorgeous. I had only ever dreamed of owning something like this, adoring the game from a young age. It was sleek, with its glass bottom making the top appear as if it was floating. Even the balls were posh, made from clear resin and set with swirls of colour in stripes or the whole thing.

"Oooh, fancy balls," I said, wagging my brows and making him laugh.

"Okay, do you want to break first?" I asked, grabbing a cue off the decorative rack and throwing him one. He caught it of course, leaning it to the wall so he could take off his jacket. Then he held out a hand and said,

"Ladies first." I curtsied, making him chuckle, before I started to position the white ball.

"Okay, but I sure hope you're not a sore loser," I commented in a cocky tone, making him scoff before saying,

"The table's in my house, doll face, trust me, I have played more times than you can... oh shit." He ended this boastful sentence the second I hit the white and knocked three balls in the pockets.

"You were saying, *doll face?*" I asked, mimicking his nickname for me. At this he started rolling up his sleeves and said,

"Right, you're in trouble now."

"Who's in trouble?" Kaiden's voice entered the room and my happiness at seeing him lasted only seconds as our eyes met, before they then shifted to Raina, who followed him inside.

"Emmeline." He said my name like a purr, making me look back to him, and he released a deep sigh before looking to his brother as if to silently communicate something.

"Oh, are we interrupting something?" she asked in a suggestive way that made Kaiden tense his jaw.

"Raina, hi... not so much interrupting, as I was just about to kick some Wrath butt, so feel free to stay and watch," I said, putting on my most friendly voice.

"Shouldn't you be back in your room?" Kaiden said, crossing his arms over his chest, making the leather of his jacket groan around his biceps. But I tried not to wince at that question and would have said something snippy when his brother intervened,

"Lighten up, brother, et arrête d'être un connard... she has been working all day and needs a break." (Translates, 'and stop being a dick' in French) Hel said, giving him a pointed look, and I was left to wonder what he had said in the middle of this sentence.

"Should we go, we do have dinner reservations?" Raina said, but Kaiden was too busy looking at me, now standing there with the cue standing up between my hands as I was using it to lean against. Then I raised my brow at him in a challenging way, waiting to see what he would do next. He didn't disappoint.

"Dinner can wait, besides, I am yet to see anyone other than myself beat my brother, so this should be entertaining," he said, making Raina pout for a second, something that went by unnoticed as he didn't even look at her. No instead, Kaiden simply removed his own jacket, placing it next to his brother's, treating me to the sight of his black shirt over dark denim. Then he moved to the other side of the room, one stylishly panelled in carved wood lacquered black. He proceeded to position himself against a sideboard, leaning back with his arms folded, showing me those strong forearms he'd left bare. He then motioned me to continue, saying,

"Well, let's see this ass kicking then, little Halo." I bit my lip the second he called me this, obviously not caring enough not to do so in front of Raina. I took a deep breath, now feeling the extra pressure. But then I knew I had it in me, so continued as it was honestly like riding a bike.

"Stripes," I chose, making Hel nod as he too stood with his cue at the ready, with a grin playing at his lips. Then, with nothing else to do but start, I lined up the shot and felt that little rush of adrenaline when it slammed right into the pocket. Then, ignoring everyone in the games room, I walked around and lined up my next shot. This time I pocketed the green and lined myself up nicely for my next ball. It was just slightly off from the pocket, so I took a little more time with this one, nicking it at the right angle so it rolled right in there.

"Well, brother, I would say that she might beat you before you even get chance at a single shot," Kaiden said with mirth in his tone, as he was clearly enjoying himself. But then, after only having two balls left, I missed the pocket and finally looked up at Kaiden, shrugging my shoulders, telling him,

"Maybe not." He grinned back at me, before motioning me over to him and I had to say that I felt a little sorry for Raina. As she was left sitting on the other side, as where Kaiden had picked there were no seats for her to take. But not wanting to make a scene by denying him, I walked over as Hel lined up his own shot.

"Where did you learn to play like that?" Kaiden asked, making me smirk.

"Caravan number six, one Mr Stanley and bored Saturdays at a worn-down clubhouse with nothing but a pool table and broken pinball machine." At this he laughed before I told him,

"Turned out Mr Stanley was once in the world championships and one game from being number one," I said with a nod of my head. Then I walked back to the table to take my shot, as Hel got stuck on his last ball. I knew then that I had him, as all I needed was one more go to clean the table. So, I set the end of my cue at the white and while blowing a loose curl out of my eyes, I looked to Kaiden. Then with his knowing smirk and raised brow looking back at me, I took the shot. But this I did being cocky enough not to break eye contact with him, as I didn't need to look at the ball to know it would fly right into the pocket. I gave him a knowing nod of my head, before telling Hel,

"Sorry, doll face," then I pocketed the black with ease, making him groan. Kaiden started clapping his large hands and Raina, feeling like she needed to act in kind, started doing the same thing. So, I dramatically held out my cue and took a bow.

"Well, damn girl," Hel muttered, making me laugh.

"Don't beat yourself up, I'm a big leagues pro." At this Kaiden straightened up and took the cue from his brother saying,

"Is that so, well then, little one, let's see how you fare against me." I was the one to raise a single brow this time and after stepping up to him, looking up I said,

"You're on, big guy." He grinned big in response to this playful banter.

"You want to break?" I asked.

"Winner breaks," he replied, granting his brother a knowing look, before nodding to Raina.

"Hey, how about me and you go get a drink while they play, this must be boring for you?" Hel said after offering her his hand.

"Oh, it's okay, I want to see who wins and cheer for Kaiden... oh no offence," Raina said to me after looking around Hel.

"None taken," I said, using the triangle to reset the balls and doing a fancy trick with the black ball, so it spun in the middle of the rest of them. Then I lined up the shot and again, knocked two in the pocket.

"Any preference?" I asked, making him shrug.

"Lady's choice." I smirked and couldn't help but reply,

*"Ever the gentleman."* He didn't miss the way I said this, mocking what Raina had said to me in the hall. He gave me a knowing look in return and as he passed behind me, he grazed my ass with the cue and said,

"Take the shot, Emmeline."

*"You got it, honey,"* I replied on a whisper, flirting back with him as again, I just couldn't seem to help it. His heated eyes told me he didn't miss it and I called,

"Stripes." Then I did my best to clear the table, only missing when he purposely stood at the pocket I was aiming for. Then he folded his arms across his chest, making his muscles bulge in the way that made my mouth dry. Damn him!

*"My turn, kitten,"* he whispered when I had growled in annoyance. I moved out of his way as he too started to clear the table, as damn but he was good. Gods, but the slamming of the balls in the pockets made me jump a little as the power behind his shots was unlike anything I had ever seen before!

But then with those biceps, could I really be surprised? I started to get panicked that he would in fact beat me, something that admittedly hadn't happened in years. So, I decided to fight fire with fire and went to stand at the pocket he was aiming at. He gave me a look as if to say he knew what I was doing. Only just before he could take the shot, I purposely leaned over, pretending to slip my shoe back on, giving him an eyeful of straight down my top.

He missed the shot.

*I grinned.*

One that turned into a sickly-sweet smile as I passed him,

now taking my last turn, and the only one I knew I would need. This time I ignored him, not even granting him a look until after I'd potted the black.

"Well, that is a first," Hel said, clapping this time, and as for Kaiden, he just nodded at me with a cunning grin playing at his lips, before offering me his hand.

*"Congratulations."* I swear he almost purred this as I put my hand in his, then he closed his fingers around my own, encasing it fully and tightening his hold when I tried to take it back.

*"Erm, thanks,"* I said shyly, and suddenly our moment was broken as Raina picked up my cue and started trying to take a shot.

"So, is it done like this, Hel?" she said, pulling back but a second after, all I saw was a line of blurred colour heading straight for me before it was suddenly…

*Lights out.*

# CHAPTER 17
# TWO DAYS

"Come back to me, little Siren." As I heard his voice, I felt lured out of my deep sleep, making me open my eyes and feel pain the second I did.

"Argh, what happened?" I asked, trying to focus as I felt Kaiden's hand smooth back my hair, before something cold touched my skin at my temple.

"You got hit in the head with the white ball," he said in a strained voice, as I knew he must have been worried.

"Jeez, do me a favour and don't let Raina play pool again," I joked, wincing as the weight of the cold compress felt like one of those cartoon anvils.

"I don't foresee she would want to after my brother snarled at her," Hel replied, making me turn to find him also in the room with us, one that I was just starting to realise wasn't the one I was used to.

"Why are we in your room?" I asked, looking back to Kaiden who was sitting next to me on the bed. He looked to his brother and jerked his head, as if to tell him silently to leave us. Something he did after first coming to me and giving me a fist to bump, making me chuckle.

"Good game, doll face."

"Thanks, sugar," I said playfully, making him grin before Kaiden grumbled,

"I will come and find you shortly." Hel simply nodded at this, as if he already knew what it would be about. Then he left us alone, making me look back to Kaiden, who still held the cold pack to my head.

"How does it look, doc?" I asked when he pulled it away to check it.

"Like it needs to be healed." I bit my lip at that, and he noticed.

"Obviously you know what that means." I nodded a little as I had written it enough times. Although it was always with him and Raina, and that caused a painful thought. Because what usually happened when a Supernatural being like Kaiden 'healed' a mortal, was they would use their blood that had regenerating properties in it. But this wasn't all that would happen as it would make the brain release a massive dose of oxytocin and dopamine, which is basically the love hormone. Ultimately, I would orgasm like a sex rocket without even being touched sexually.

"I think I will keep the lump," I said, shifting off the bed and making him reach for me, stopping me from walking away with a hold on my hand. I looked back at him when he said my name.

"Emmeline."

"We can't," I told him, pulling my hand from his and making him sigh.

"The fuck we can't," he said, getting to his feet and

following me down the steps into the living space, one that I didn't want to be in right now.

"It's not…"

"I swear if you say it's not right, one more time," he growled.

"You will what? Make me your prisoner and force me to sleep in your arms every night?" I threw back at him, hating how hurt he looked at that, despite masking it quickly with a frown.

"Look, I don't have it in me to do this again," I said, making him cross his arms over his chest and stare down at me.

"So, you still wish to punish me over what I said to you, even after I apologised. As I have to say, Emmeline, I didn't take you for someone unforgiving and cruel." At this I whipped around to face him and told him all the things I shouldn't do, letting my anger ignite this time.

"I am not punishing you!"

"No? Then perhaps you should ask yourself why you have been cold and distant with me, something you admitted to my brother before admitting it to me. I believe your exact words were, *I have been giving him a hard time lately.*"

"Oh great, nice to know saying things in confidence is still a thing," I muttered sarcastically.

"You should not have any secrets with me," he stated firmly.

"No, and does that mean the same thing for you?" I asked foolishly.

"I keep nothing from you," he stated, and oh boy did he just do it!

"Oh, so I didn't walk to your office the other night to

hear you admit to your brother that you do have feelings for Raina and want to claim me quickly as you think it will stop them growing!" I shouted, throwing the cold pack to the floor in my anger. At this he looked shocked before he closed his eyes whispering,

*"You were there?"*

"Oh yeah, I was there!" I snapped.

"Why?" he asked, making me frown, before shaking my head a little, wondering what that had to do with anything!

"It doesn't matter why!" I snapped.

"The fuck it doesn't, now tell me why!" he said, changing the subject and making this about me, hence why I yelled at him,

"No!"

"Tell me!" he shouted back.

"I SAID NO!" I screamed at him this time, before storming from the room and slamming the door, running back to the room I now considered my own. I heard the roar of anger behind me before the growl.

"Fuck!" Then I glanced behind to find myself being stalked by one very angry Demon. Which was why I started running faster. Not that this did me any good as suddenly an arm banded around my waist, and I was lifted right off my running feet.

*"Running only makes me want you more!"* he growled dangerously in my ear before he turned and was walking me back to his own room, making me try to fight against him.

"Put me down!" I shouted, trying to move his arm, digging my nails into his skin and making him nip at my neck in warning. Then he walked straight into his room and

144

the moment he put me down, I tried to run from him. This was when he snagged the back of my sweater, and yanked me hard enough that I was forced to walk backwards. Then I found my back to the wall and one hungry, angry male surrounding me before my wrists were shackled and held above me.

"Let me go! I am not playing!" I shouted, making him transfer both my wrists into one, pinning my hands to the wall with ease. Then he took a deep, calming breath now that he had me where he wanted me.

*"I have not even started playing with you,"* he warned before shocking me as he bit into the palm of his hand. I gasped for breath when he brought forth a single claw, one he lifted to the top of my head. I started shaking it from side to side, as his own blood dripped down his wrist.

"STOP!" he roared in his Demonic voice, making me wince and hold still, because admittedly, I was scared. Then he took another calming breath and went back to the task of healing me, first by nicking the lump, making me cry out at the sting.

After this he placed his bleeding palm to my new cut, doing this so his blood could now get into my own system. I tried to knee him in the balls, something he protected himself against as he turned side on, so his thigh took the hit. Then he pressed himself further into me, stopping me from trying that again.

"Play at being feisty, sweetheart? *I fucking like it!"* he growled, making me turn my face away as he tried to kiss me. He groaned against my cheek and when I tried to move my head, he whispered more softly this time,

*"Still for me now, just give it time… please, Emmeline."* He whispered this last part, and I couldn't do anything but what he asked, as the way he said please just got to me every time.

"Good Gi…"

"Don't say it, Kaiden," I threatened as he was about to praise me, and he released a deep sigh before telling me,

"Alright, sweetheart… now just let go and let it happen… that's it… I've got you now," he said, responding to the way I tensed in his arms, feeling it already starting to take effect and soon I was screaming out my release.

"AHHH OOOHHH FUCK!" I bellowed this as one of the most powerful orgasms ripped through me when I wasn't even expecting it to happen that quickly. I felt him tighten his hold on my wrists as my legs ceased to be able to hold me any longer. Then suddenly I was tipped up over his shoulder and this time, I didn't even try and fight him. I just felt him carry me to the bed and lower me down, reaching his hand up and supporting my back. Then he cupped my head so he could put me down even more gently. After this I felt him smooth back my hair from my face, using the hand that wasn't covered in blood, a hand that was already healed.

Speaking of healing,

"I was not about to let you go without first ridding you of your injury… *I don't like seeing my girl hurt."* He whispered this last part down over my neck, making me suck in a deep breath.

"Can I go back to my room now?" I asked in a calm voice, making him grumble.

"Alright, little one, we will continue to play this your

way for now, but just so as you know, you have two days left before you will be in this bed... *where you will remain,"* he told me, caressing a gentle thumb over my lips and watching the way I captured the bottom one in between my teeth, making him grin. Then he allowed me to get off the bed this time, now it was on his terms and honestly, I wasn't sure how I felt about that. I wasn't sure how I felt about him forcing the issue of healing me.

But then I remembered what his brother had said, about how he was struggling with all these new emotions. I guess for a being like Wrath, that had only known this life as a lord and leader, used to getting whatever he wanted, I was... *different.*

I was the one element in his life that he couldn't control, no matter how much he tried. No matter how much he was used to getting his own way. I was the exception to his rule. The thorn he couldn't just yank out and be done with. Because I had clearly gotten under his skin and according to him, was staying there for the foreseeable future.

He stood next to me and after first wiping the blood off his hand with the T-shirt he wore, he took my hand in his and this time, he walked me calmly back to my room, doing so in silence. I had to admit, that I felt better and more comforted the second I was inside, still not feeling as if I belonged in Kaiden's personal space. Especially not after hearing him say to Hel how he admitted that he felt something for Raina.

"I will give you some time alone and be back to check on you later." I nodded at this but when I didn't respond the way he wanted me to, he hooked my chin and forced me to look up at him. After this he granted me a tender kiss that was one, for once, he didn't deepen into something more. Then he told me,

"Remember what I said, Emmeline, just two more days and then..." he paused to whisper this single vow over my lips...

*"...You're mine."*

## CHAPTER 18
# LIES AND WISHES

The moment he said this, he left me alone. Now I was feeling so many emotions it was hard to pinpoint just one. I wanted him to want me. I wanted him to pick me, of course I did. I never wanted anything more in my entire life. But I didn't want it at the expense of his happiness because this was no longer about Raina.

And if I was honest with myself.

*It never had been.*

Because in truth, I didn't know her. But then, I had never even tried. I had been too bitter, too jealous, too emotional to even try and see this from her point. I had been the one to reach out to her, believing that there was a chance she could have been just another name that matched. I had no idea it would actually turn out to be as I had thought. And now, I was drowning in regret, because in the time I had been here, I had just fallen more in love with Kaiden.

Honestly, I had no idea how I would ever move on from this. I had tried not to even think about it, allowing his affections returned to make me believe and hope like I never had before. His tender words of need and want and care had drawn me in and kept me safely in his comforting net all this time.

His words had kept me tethered to the heart of him and I never wanted to be set free of it. I didn't want him to wake one day and cut that cord. I didn't want to be set free.

*Free of him.*

Naturally, these turbulent thoughts didn't make it easy to rest and the time Kaiden thought I needed was more like torture as my mind had never been so confused. Which was most likely why I made the horrible decision to try and speak with Raina the next chance I got. Although I had to wonder when, if any, the next opportunity would be.

Because, when hearing the usual lock sliding home as soon as Kaiden had closed the door, it didn't give me much hope that this would happen. Which was why I was really confused when I heard the door unlocking, holding my breath as I expected Kaiden to walk through it a second later.

However, this didn't happen.

I frowned wondering what was going on, so I got to my feet and went to investigate. Roger hissed as he usually did, making me hiss back,

"Yeah well, I was expecting a cat I could stroke without wanting to rip my face off, so what you gonna do but reap what you sow, buddy?" I said, making him turn his back to me and basically give me the proverbial kitty finger. Then I walked to the door and stuck my head out when it opened.

"Hello?" I called out softly, not wanting to shout. There was nothing there, making me mutter,

"That's weird." I looked back to the room unsure of what

to do, knowing that Kaiden might be pissed if he thought I was trying to run, especially after what had just happened between us. But then, it wasn't as though I was going to be stupid enough to go walking around outside, so really, if I stayed away from any exits, then what was the harm? After all, he had left it open once and I hadn't run, surely this should be enough to convince him should he find me wandering around.

I mean, what was he going to do if he did decide he wanted to claim me? Keep me locked to a ball and chain, twisting the usual saying on its head? He would have to start trusting me at some point.

"Fuck it," I said before stepping out into the hallway and listening out for any voices. I continued on, first walking one way and then the other. Until finally I walked down the stairs and travelled the same way that Hel had shown me earlier. Maybe a quick stop at the library would give me something to do, as solitaire on my laptop was getting old now.

I turned another corner, wondering if I would need a map of this place soon, as I had stopped to get my bearings twice. But then I heard voices from up the hall.

No, not voices, just one…

*Raina's.*

"I am telling you, it's not working like we thought it would… well, tell him to act quicker and I will do my part," she said, keeping her voice low, and I could tell now that she was on the phone as no one replied.

"Well, can't you make it stronger? I've only got… wait, is someone there?" She pushed the door open to find me standing there and I tried to act natural.

"I will call you back," she snapped angrily, hanging up the phone and walking back inside.

"Didn't anyone ever tell you not to eavesdrop on people's private conversations?" her snippy voice said, making me frown.

"Erm, I wasn't, I just arrived when you opened the door." I defended myself, making her scoff and I had to say, she wasn't as warm and friendly as she had been, making me realise now that it had all been an act.

"Look Emma…"

"It's Emmeline."

"Yeah whatever. Look, I get this is difficult seeing as you got us together and all, but you're making this really hard on Kaiden, he just wants to be with me, but feels like he owes you or something, I don't know… can't you just leave so we can be together…? All you're doing is hurting him, can't you see that?" At this I was so shocked I even took a step back, needing a wall to support me.

"He… he didn't say that," I stuttered, making her sigh dramatically.

"Actually, he did, something about being worried you would go back to writing your little stories or whatever." I actually gasped at this and started shaking my head.

"No, he wouldn't… he wouldn't say that!" I shouted this last part, making her grin… actually fucking grin! Oh, and I soon knew why, as she said even louder this time,

"Look, I like you, Emmeline, but like I keep telling you, I will not help you escape, I couldn't do that to Kai, I won't betray his trust and you shouldn't either!"

"What the…? Kaiden!" I shouted the second the door burst open and Kaiden was there looking beyond furious.

*He had heard all of her lies.*

"Kaiden, I…" I started to try and say when he sliced an angry hand down to his side.

*"Silence!"* he suddenly roared down at me, making me flinch back.

"I'm so sorry you had to hear it like this, Kai, she just wouldn't stop asking for my help. I kept saying no but there is only so much I can take. I was going to tell you tonight," Raina said, making me suck in a stunned breath before stammering out,

*"But… but that's not what…"* he snapped his head back to me and growled, making me stop. Then I watched as he walked to Raina, put a hand on her shoulder and said,

"Thank you for the loyalty you show, it means a great deal to me." At this I felt sickened by the sight as she leaned her cheek against his hand and said,

"I would do anything for you, my darling." At this I could take no more as a sob tore from me and I ran from the room, pushing past Hel the moment I did.

"Whoa, where's the fire?" he asked but I kept running, hearing Kaiden and Hel behind me,

"Kai?"

"I don't have time to explain, ask Raina, *for I've got a prisoner to deal with!"* I heard him snarl, making me cry even harder. I quickly got to my room, only doing so this time as Kaiden didn't chase after me, no… *he slowly stalked me.* Hunted me like prey. Prey that he thought had been trying to escape all this time.

"THAT BITCH!" I suddenly screamed at the ceiling while bending my knees and clenching my fists at my sides. Gods, I was so fucking angry! She had lied, she had fucking lied through her teeth. And all to get me out of the picture. All so that Kaiden would hear everything she said but how had she known he was there...? Had she heard him approaching when I missed it?

*She had totally played me!*

I nearly jumped out of my skin when I heard the door slam behind me. I swallowed hard before turning to the furious face of Wrath.

"I can explain," I tried but it was no use, I knew that the moment he shouted at me,

"How the fuck did you get out of your room!?"

"You're not going to believe me," I told him, trying to keep myself calm in hopes that he would do the same.

"Tell me how?!" he bellowed again.

"It was opened, I don't know how," I tried in vain as he shouted,

"Bullshit!" I flinched at that.

"I swear it to you, someone opened it and I just..."

"STOP FUCKING LYING TO ME!" he roared, making me take a few steps back. Then I narrowed my gaze, throwing my fists back behind me as I leaned forward.

"DON'T FUCKING SHOUT AT ME!" I screamed back, letting my rage fuel my response. Which was when we ended up panting, both of us now taking the time to breathe through our joint anger.

"I don't know what it is I can do anymore, Emmeline," he said, dragging a hand down his face, and I took a deep breath.

"I am telling you the truth, I swear, I didn't open that door, Kaiden," I replied, making him look up from the floor and say,

"I want to believe you but after what Raina said…"

"So you would believe her over me?!" I said in outrage.

"She has never run from me before and fucking succeeded!" he snapped back, and I winced at that.

"You knew why I ran!" I said, trying for reason this time.

"Yes, and now you run because you know I will claim you, despite all your fucking efforts at trying to push me into the arms of another woman!" he threw back, hitting his mark just right, seeing as I had been feeling shit about the whole thing since it began.

"No, that's not it and if you would just listen…"

"Oh, but all I have done is listen to you and look where it has brought us! If you had just fucking trusted me in the first place, then none of this would have happened and you…" he stopped himself just in time, forcing me to press for it.

"What?!"

"YOU WOULD BE MINE!" his Demon roared this time, and in that moment, I knew how close to the edge he was. So, I took a deep breath, trying to calm my own temper in hopes of calming his.

"I know you think this is me pushing you away, but I promise you…"

"Promise me? Promise me what, Emmeline!? More chances to give you to run!?" he yelled, making me sigh in frustration.

"I didn't try and run, and I didn't open that fucking door," I snapped before walking to it and slamming it shut but fuck me, I couldn't believe then what I found. Because in the door was a long piece of metal that fell out of the lock the moment I slammed it. Gods, but it looked like a bent fork, made like that for only one purpose. I frowned down at where it had fallen on the floor and Kaiden did the same.

"I…I…" I started to say the moment he opened his hand, making it fly from the floor and into his palm.

"Kaiden, I…" At this he snarled,

*"I am done with your lies, but no more!"* I bit my lip at that and felt the tears started to build up. Then I watched as he crushed the fork in his hand.

*"No more, Emmeline,"* he said, throwing the mangled piece of metal to the floor with an angry slash of his hand. I jumped back as it bounced, making me cry out a little. Then he stormed towards the door and as he passed me, I reached out and grabbed his arm, trying to stop him. He snarled down at me, making me let him go, and all I could do was whisper his name,

*"Kaiden, please."* He closed his eyes and then said the words that shot straight to my heart…

*"Tonight, you get your wish."*

## CHAPTER 19
# BLACK WATER RISING

After he left, I fell to the floor crying, flinching when I heard the lock click and I swear this time, the sound echoed in the room. I was utterly devastated, as I didn't know what hurt more, the fact that he didn't believe me or what he said to me before he left.

What did that even mean, that tonight I would get my wish? Did he mean to let me go or did he mean that he would pick Raina and tonight he would claim her?!

*"Oh Gods, but what have I done?"* I cried out this time and in the end, I managed to calm myself enough to drag my ass into bed. I then curled up on myself and tried to cry myself to sleep. Because I couldn't bear the idea of what he could be doing now. Had he taken her to his room? Was he seconds away from forgetting me forever, claiming her as I had pushed him to do?

It was no wonder I spent hours sobbing, feeling sorry for myself and wallowing in my pain. And what was worse, was that Raina was clearly not what she made herself out to be. Who had she been talking to on the phone, and was she trying to somehow trap Kaiden? Gods, but was she even the real Raina? Of course, I knew she was the girl I always saw in my dreams, so how I was to explain that I didn't know? Yet still, was that enough to make her Kaiden's Siren?

I had once believed it was, but now… well, *I wasn't so sure.* What if he could be making a terrible mistake right now? What if Kaiden's enemy, Dagon was involved? What if this was all a trap?

I tossed and turned and, in the end, I had no idea how much sleep I'd had, if it was hours or only five minutes. Either way, I woke with a start the moment I heard the door unlock, feeling my entire body relax as Kaiden had finally come back to me. Now I just needed to get him to understand, to explain my side and force him to listen. I had no clue how that stupid fork had gotten into the lock, but one thing was for sure, and that was someone was going to a lot of trouble to try to get me out the way.

It clearly hadn't been Raina as she didn't seem to be expecting me, despite her certainly knowing the right shit to say when Kaiden turned up. So what the Hell was going on?

*"Kaiden?"* I asked, sitting up when I didn't hear him enter the room, however, this ended on a scream as a figure in a black cloak was suddenly standing at the end of the bed. Although, my scream didn't last long as I was suddenly hit with something across my face. This happened with so much force that it knocked me to the floor from the bed.

"Ahhh!" I cried out as pain exploded across my cheek and up my arm as I fell on it at a funny angle. I never had a chance to get away, as suddenly my hair was grabbed in a fist. Then, as I fought to be freed, I was being dragged across the floor towards the balcony. I reached up and grabbed the person's wrists, trying to get them to let me go and even more pain assaulted me as it felt as if my hair was about to be torn from my scalp.

"Let go of me!" I shouted before I was kicked in the stomach, making me wheeze out a pained breath, coughing through it. Then all too soon, I was at the balustrades being yanked up to my feet. But as the person behind me was trying to push me off the edge, I kicked my feet up in my panic to save myself the fall to my death.

I scrambled for leverage to push back, using my foot on one of the large stone urns that decorated the tops of the waist-height pillars. I pushed backwards as hard as I could, at the same time the strength of the person behind me was gaining more distance. I cried out as I got closer to the edge, making my knees bend even more.

"NO! STOP THIS!" I shouted, but it was no use as one more push was all it took, and the urn finally gave way. It shifted from its plinth and slid to the edge before it tipped completely off it. I heard the crashing of glass below as it smashed its way through the roof that covered the pool and soon, I could do nothing as I too…

*Followed it.*

I screamed as I fell, remembering looking up at the black figure above as they watched me falling, making sure their victim died as intended. I suddenly landed in the water and that was when I realised…

It was just as they intended for me to.

They somehow knew I couldn't swim out of my depth and right now, I was very much as out of my depth as I could get. I hit the back of my head on the bottom of the pool, making me cry out under water, losing what precious air I did have in my lungs when I went under.

The water around me swirled with ribbons of blood, making it look black in the dark room surrounding me, floating inches from my face. I could feel the glass I landed on slice at my skin, and I winced in even more pain, knowing that I was going to drown if I didn't at least try and make it to the surface. Then finally, as the watery figure of my killer above finally thought I had died, and left the scene of the crime, I started to move.

Come on, Emme! You fucking know how to swim, don't let the fear win! *Don't let fear fucking kill you!* I screamed in my own mind at this, knowing I just needed to make it to the side. I just needed to reach the surface and take a breath!

*Just one fucking breath!*

I started to reach up, moving my arms and fighting for life against the pain, against the blood I'd lost. I pulled and pulled, reaching up and pushing down, I knew how to do this. My head suddenly burst free of the surface, and I dragged in lungs full of air, saving myself from drowning just that little bit longer. I started moving my arms, trying to get myself to the side, but then a memory assaulted me.

Falling backwards off the dock into the lake. Screaming out for my Nanna as my back hit the water. Everything looked so dark down there, with black clouds rolling in above. I had been caught in a thunderstorm, in a rush to gather up my things as rain started to pour around me. I had slipped in my haste. I remember watching the rain hitting the surface above me, trying in vain to reach up for it. Until a hand suddenly saved me.

Where was that hand now?

In my panic, I went under again. But I couldn't stay there, or this time, I would really die. So I started kicking my legs, and when I reached the surface, I used the last of my air to scream to the only person I knew who could save me now. The only hand that could reach me in time. Because I had his blood inside me. I had therefore made the slightest connection to him.

It would have to be enough.

*It had to be.*

"KAIDEN, HELP ME!" I screamed as loud as I could before going under for a second time. This time though, I had no air left and worse still, I had no time left either. I had tried to save myself and failed. Now all I could hope for was that when Kaiden eventually found me, that he wouldn't feel like he'd failed too. I didn't want him to suffer the pain of that.

*The pain of losing his Siren.*

I finally let the dark water take me, feeling myself falling deeper under as I had nothing left in me to fight with. The person on the balcony had taken it all from me. And what was worse, I never got to tell Kaiden how I really felt...

I never got to say the words...

*I love you.*

I closed my eyes just as a shadow appeared above me like a Dark Angel of Death finally arriving to take me. I knew then, it was time. Time to say goodbye. I felt the water moving, swirling around me as if the Angel had just jumped in and grabbed hold of my weightless body floating in the water. Then I felt myself rising quickly, until cold was all I felt.

My mind was strangely detached from the rest of my

body as all I could hear was a strange echoing sound, like my name was being called at the end of a very long tunnel. Then suddenly I felt pain as I was ripped away from wherever my mind had been heading and I came back to my broken body with a start. I choked up water, coughing through the burn. But as I opened my eyes, the first sight I saw was Kaiden's hands above me, as if he had been the one to drag the water out of my lungs with his powers.

"Emmeline!" he shouted, cradling me in his arms, holding me to him as if he was afraid I would be ripped from his life.

"What happened?!" I faintly heard Hel's unnerved voice.

"I don't fucking know! I am going to heal what I can, but she needs a hospital!" Kaiden snapped angrily... no not angrily...

*Panicked.*

I felt myself losing my sense of reality at that point, doing so to the desperate sounds of Kaiden's,

"Stay with me, Emmeline! Stay with me! Gods, please stay with me... *with me... my Siren.*" I knew then that I must have been dreaming, as he couldn't have just made that claim. That's when I realised, as I fell back into the sweet oblivion of my dreams, that at least I got to die hearing his voice one more time.

*The voice of my Enforcer.*

## CHAPTER 20
# CUTTING THE CORD

I don't know why, but my dreams twisted from good to bad. One moment I was peacefully finding myself in Kaiden's arms with him whispering soothing words down at me. His caring and tender voice, like a healing balm upon my soul, was one I clung onto for as long as possible.

But then that same darkness started to swirl around me like a silent storm trying to take me under. I would see a dark figure leaning over me, trying once more to take my life. A person next to my bed, flashing in and out of being cloaked at the bottom of it and then next to me in a light room, reaching for some beeping machine. Then a furious voice arguing as if someone was stopping the person from hurting me. A malicious growl saying now wasn't the time. That I was worth too much alive.

After this I experienced some peace, every now and again feeling my hand being held, or my hair being tucked gently behind my ear. A tender caress down my cheek or even a kiss upon my forehead were the moments I clung to the most. But eventually, reality seeped its way back into my subconscious mind and I was opening my eyes to find my world was no longer black.

I looked down at my hand to find a head resting next to it, and the moment I saw twisted dreads mixed with smooth strands of dark hair pulled back into a Viking style, I knew who it was that was by my bedside. I glanced up to the side, seeing machines beeping, showing my vitals and then a bag of fluids that connected to my hand.

*I was in hospital.*

Knowing this, I sighed and moved my fingers across his cheek, making him wake suddenly.

*"Emmeline?"* He whispered my name and I swear the hope in his voice broke my heart a little, knowing that with just one look in those green eyes, he had been worried for me.

*"Thank the Gods,"* he said as if on a personal prayer.

*"Hey,"* I croaked, making him sit up and quickly get me some water, using the straw there to put to my lips.

"Here, drink this," he told me softly, rising from his chair and standing over me. I did as he asked, feeling better as it soothed my scratchy throat.

"What happened?" I asked, making him wince before telling me,

*"You... fell."* The way he said it, in such a pained way, I could tell there was something he wasn't telling me, but I couldn't remember what happened.

"Don't think about it for now, just sleep, you need rest as your body heals." I frowned as he reached above me and pressed a button.

"But I... I need to know what..."

"Ssshh now, you're safe and that's all that matters," he

interrupted. But before I could try again, the door opened and a pretty, dark haired nurse entered who had one of the kindest smiles I had ever seen.

"Well, look who woke up," she said in a cheery way as she walked over and started checking my vitals.

"Any pain?" she asked, making me shake my head but Kaiden intervened and said,

*"She needs to rest."* The way he said this conveyed something to the nurse and before I knew it, she was doing something with the IV fluids. A few moments after this, I was feeling really drowsy, making me realise what they had done.

"But I don't want to…"

"Sleep, Emmeline, sleep now and I will protect you… I will watch over you…"

*"While I still can."*

☿

After this tender moment between us, I woke up the next day, but Kaiden wasn't there sitting next to my bed like last time. There was no one holding my hand.

*I was alone.*

This was when things started to piece back together. Kaiden had saved me from drowning. He had been the one to get me out of the pool. But how had I got there? I honestly couldn't remember.

"Hey, pretty girl, she's awake again!" the same cheery nurse said, walking into the room I was in. I could also make her out better this time as my head felt somewhat clearer. She was a few inches taller than me and was naturally slim at the waist, creating a curved flare to her hips. But it was her smile that was really killer, as she reminded me of Julia Roberts, with the endearing grin that you couldn't help but match with one of your own. An infectious smile that no doubt helped put patients at ease, no matter what she did. She also had a pair of dimples that added to the cuteness that swung more to beautiful than just charming. Her bright hazel eyes seemed almost playful, and I swear this girl most likely woke up smiling at the world. And why wouldn't she, looking like that? Her cheekbones alone made me want to weep.

"Hey," I said before asking quickly,

"There was a man here before…"

"Mr West, yes, he was here and man alive, but I didn't think he was ever going to leave your bedside. One of the other nurses made the mistake of suggesting he leave to get some rest and I swear he actually growled!" she said laughing, and if I thought Raina had a sing-song voice, then this girl put that blonde to shame. But wait, Raina… *hadn't something happened between us?*

"But I told them to leave him be, besides, he was so big and scary I don't think anyone was brave enough to go near him after that."

"That's sounds like Kaiden," I muttered, making her grin at me… again, it was blinding.

"Well, I am Emily and was told you're Emmeline, so it's nice to meet you." I grinned back as she was so nice, making me reply in earnest,

"Likewise."

"I have to say, we were all concerned for a time there as we didn't think you were going to wake up… must have been good dreams, yeh?" she told me, wagging her dark shapely brows, making me ask,

"How long was I asleep for?"

"You were brought in four days ago," she said, shocking me.

"But don't worry, all has been taken care of," she added, making me frown.

"What do you mean?"

"Well, that man, the big dude who brought you in, he paid the bill already, had clothes brought and said that there would be a car waiting for you."

"A car?" I asked as her words confused me, quickly making me ask,

"Where is he now?"

"Hey, don't worry, I am sure he will be back soon. How about I go ring and check, yeah? He told me to call him when you woke anyway," she said looking concerned as clearly, I was struggling with all of this.

"You mean he's not here… he… *he left the hospital?*" I asked painfully, and she saw it, gripping my shoulder and reminding me,

"I'm sure he just popped home to get changed, grab something to eat, after all, he didn't leave your side until you woke last night. He was so worried, I could tell." I relaxed back at this, telling her,

"Yeah, you're probably right." But even as I said the words, I knew something was wrong. Kaiden wouldn't have left me, not even for a second… *would he?*

"Hey, Emily… Thank you," I said before she left the room, making her grin and say,

"Sure thing, sugar, now you rest up and I will go ring

that boyfriend of yours for you." I nodded, not correcting her, as really, what was the point? No, instead I let my head fall back, remembering that I should be hurt there, as the memory of hitting it on the bottom of the pool came to me.

*Had he healed me?*

All that glass, and yet there wasn't a single mark on me. He must have saved me from my injuries as well. But then I couldn't help but ask, why wasn't he here now?

*"Where are you, Kaiden?"* I muttered aloud, looking to the window and seeing the rain lashing against it, mirroring my mood.

In the end, my questions as to why, would have to wait as a doctor came in shortly after to examine me. He told me that I was fine to be discharged and that I could get dressed after a nurse had taken out my IV and catheter. Unfortunately, it was another nurse that did it this time, so I couldn't ask if they had got in contact with Kaiden.

So, with little else to do, I got up and dressed in the new clothes that had been bought for me by someone I didn't know. A pair of soft cream leggings, a dark red strappy top and big knitted sweater in a toffee and oatmeal colour. Oh, and a pair of high heel boots that I don't know why, but just the sight of them made me want to cry.

*Where was Kaiden?*

Surely, he had been told I was awake by now? I just didn't get it. But with nothing else to do but get myself sorted, I used the bathroom. I also brushed my teeth, ran my fingers through my tangle of curls best I could and washed my face, wishing I had taken the time to shower. But seeing as I wanted to be ready for when Kaiden turned up, I hadn't bothered. Now I was wondering who I was actually waiting for, as the same nurse that had taken out my IV came into tell me that there was a car waiting for me downstairs.

"But I am waiting for a man, a Mr Wra... I mean, West," I said, and she told me,

"I have no idea, they just rang up to tell us about the car," she replied, making me wince.

"Oh, okay," I said, shaking my head a little as if trying to make sense of it all. But with nothing else to do but leave, I walked out into the hallway, thankfully bumping straight into Emily.

"Emmeline! I was just on my way to see you, sorry I was swamped with a patient, but I managed to get hold of Mr West, although I was surprised when he told me to tell you that he was sending a car... I'm sorry, I thought he would be here."

"So, he's not coming?" I asked in a pained way, not understanding why.

"No, but he did say he would meet you at home." I frowned at that and couldn't help but feel disappointed that he wouldn't even come here to take me home himself.

"Hey, don't worry, I'm sure something super important came up," she said, trying to make me feel better, and I had to thank her for that.

"Take it easy now, no late-night swimming, yeah?" she said, giving me a thumbs up as she walked away backwards. After that I made my way to the exit, soon finding a limo waiting for me, parked where it shouldn't but waiting all the same. I even found myself hoping that I would find him sitting inside... *but no.*

*Again, I was alone.*

That's when that bad feeling grew into dread and then

into outright panic, especially when I realised we weren't driving out of the city like we should be.

"Are we going to Lexington?" I asked the driver who told me,

"No, my Lord Wrath wanted me to take you home." I frowned at this, telling him,

"But I don't live in the city." He ignored this and continued driving regardless, making his way to a fancy apartment building opposite central park.

"Here you go, miss, the front desk is expecting you," he told me, making me frown up at the building before my door was opened by a fancy doorman.

"Miss Raidne?" he asked as I got out of the car, still totally confused as to what was going on.

"Yes, that's me," I said when he still looked as if he was waiting for my answer.

"Right this way, Miss," he said, prompting me to follow him, and when he showed me to the fancy front desk in a lobby decorated entirely in black and white, I did as I was told, still in a daze of disbelief. A cheery woman behind a glass desk that held nothing but a computer screen, smiled at me in greeting.

"Ah, Miss Raidne, lovely to finally meet you, I have your keys here for your apartment." I frowned at the smart business woman who wore a suit as if she had come out of the womb looking like she was born to play an extra from the Devil wears Prada.

"My apartment, no, there must be some mistake, I don't live…" I started to say, making her tell me quickly,

"Mr West said that he would explain everything, I believe he is up there waiting for you."

"Wait, Kaiden is here?!" I shouted, shocking her before she slid the envelope over to me.

"I believe everything you need is in there. The elevators are just around the corner, and Mr West said you would already know the code that will take you directly to the penthouse." I shook my head a little, feeling like my world was quickly spinning out of control.

"I'm sorry, the penthouse?"

"Yes, I believe Mr West spared no expense." I frowned for what felt like the millionth time since waking, and walked away after thanking her. I found the elevators and now that I knew Kaiden was up there, I was eager to get to him. Eager to find out what the Hell was going on. So, after putting in the only code I could think of, being the same as the one to get into Sins, I travelled up to the top.

*"He spared no expense?"* I questioned aloud. Then, when the elevator doors opened, I stepped into another lobby, one smaller this time before reaching for the gold handle. I actually held my breath before opening the door and only a moment after walking inside, I sucked in a quick breath...

*There he was.*

Kaiden Wrath was standing with his back to me, staring out onto the view of central park by the wall of windows that flooded the open plan living space in daylight. One darkened slightly by the rain that continued to batter against another window this time.

"Kaiden!" I shouted his name and started off running across the large room, before stopping the moment he turned to face me, giving me hard eyes. I swear that look alone had the power to freeze the blood in my veins! It most definitely had the strength to have me stop suddenly, now rooted to the spot, no longer easy about getting closer to him.

The same hard man that I had first seen that day in the elevator, the Demon overlord was back, and as for me, I no longer meant the same to him as I once had. I knew with that one look alone.

"Emmeline." He said my name without feeling, and it was the first time I had ever heard it spoken like that before.

"Kaiden, I don't..."

"You will find you have everything you need in that envelope. The kitchen has been stocked, you have new credit cards, your clothes hang in your closet..." he stated like he was in some kind of business meeting, telling the world how it should be run.

"Closet? Wait, is this... is this my new home?" I asked but he ignored me and went on to say,

"Your cat will be delivered here shortly."

"Kaiden, I don't understand, what is all this?" I asked almost breathlessly.

"Everything has been taken care of, as per your wishes," he stated firmly.

"My wishes? I never wished for this?" I told him, making him sigh as if this was all very taxing on him.

"Don't make this harder than it has to be. It is a promise I made and one I intend to keep," he told me reaching for his jacket, and I watched dumbfounded as he put it on. He was going to leave me.

*"Wait, you're leaving?!"*

"I don't see the point in prolonging this, do you?" he asked, snapping this out as though what was happening now was obvious.

"Prolonging what, you dumping me here in your modern castle to rot away!"

"I would hardly call the life I am giving you rotting away," he snapped, making me shout back,

"Then what would you call it?!"

*"Living a life...* unlike what you tried to achieve!" he shouted this time, shocking me enough that my mouth dropped.

"I...I don't..."

"No, you didn't. You didn't think. Well, now the choice has been taken from you and made, for make no mistakes, there is no going back from this now," he warned, making me narrow my eyes at him.

"Going back from what?" I asked, totally confused as to why he was acting like this. But this was when he totally rocked me to my core.

*"Trying to kill yourself,"* he stated, after closing his eyes briefly, showing me the first shred of emotion other than shouting at me.

"I did what?!" I screeched.

"Don't play dumb now, are you really trying to tell me that you don't remember?" I was so utterly astounded that I started shaking my head, walking backwards and holding out a shaky hand to him as tears blurred my vision.

"I don't... I didn't... I wouldn't do that. I wouldn't fucking do that, Kaiden!" I shouted this last part before he released a deep sigh, then he reached for my own laptop off the coffee table, picked it up and opened it up, before handing it to me.

"Press play when I leave, *for I can't watch it again."* He snarled this last part, and I could tell it was said in utter pain.

I looked down at my laptop to see that it was paused on a video footage, one I didn't dare press play on. I was too fucking terrified to.

"Kaiden, this isn't…"

"Oh, but it is, Emmeline," he said, nodding down at the laptop in my shaky hands.

"That is exactly what happened in your last and final attempt to escape me. Well, consider it message received, *loud and fucking clear*. What is it that my brother told me you said to him once, if you love something, let it go… well, consider this me letting you go and, *Emme… I don't expect you back,"* he said, now walking towards the door, making me cry out his name, dropping the laptop to the couch.

"Kaiden, wait!"

"No! Not this time, Emmeline."

*"But that's not how the saying goes,"* I told him in a pained, quiet voice, making his shoulders drop just as he reached for the door. Then he looked back at me and said his final goodbye and with it, the final crack to my heart, destroying me completely this time.

"It does in this story, for I have already found my Siren and now I know with certainty…"

*"…it's not you."*

## CHAPTER 21
## THE COST OF CALLING

After he said this, he left and as soon as I heard the door close, I fell to my knees and broke down into pieces. I sobbed uncontrollably, covering my face and pouring every single emotion of pain I felt in that moment as the tears just wouldn't stop.

The pain just wouldn't stop.

I quickly grabbed for my laptop and after taking a shuddered breath, I forced myself the bravery needed to press play. Because I had to know what he saw. I had to see what it was he thought I had done. An act that broke his heart and pushed him into the arms of Raina for good. Gods, but if only I could remember that night! Well, there was only one way of doing that, and that was by pressing play. But as soon as I did this, I instantly wished that I hadn't!

I grabbed the sides of my laptop and cried out,

"NO! No, no, no, no! I wouldn't have done this! It's a fucking lie! IT'S A LIE!" I screamed, throwing my laptop across the room, smashing it into the kitchen island before throwing myself down on the couch and crying out in agony.

I wouldn't have done that! I wouldn't have fucking jumped! But then why was there video surveillance of me pushing the urn off first before climbing the balustrades and throwing myself off them.

*Why?!*

I wouldn't have done that!

Gods, but no wonder he fucking hated me! He thought that I would rather kill myself than be with him. How could he believe that? Didn't he know that I loved him?! The very reason I had done all of this. It had all been done for my love of him. But then what if he now thought I had been trying to push him into Raina's arms all along because I didn't want to be his Siren. That I had *never* wanted to be his Siren? Gods, is that what he thought?

Did he not know me at all?!

Well, it didn't matter now. Nothing mattered anymore. As I had lost him. I had lost the only man I had ever loved and what was worst of all, I had no idea why. Why I had done something so foolish, when deep in my heart I knew I never would have been capable of that. Not when I knew what I would be leaving behind. Because even if he had chosen Raina over me, I would rather live in a world where I knew Kaiden was happy than die in one knowing I had hurt him with my last selfish act on Earth.

*It wasn't like me at all!*

I don't know how long I cried for in the end, but the next time I raised my head was when the doorbell rang, making me call out his name,

"Kaiden!" I then ran to the door and tore it open, but when I saw it was Boaz holding my cat carrier, I burst into tears. In fact, he had to drop my cat and catch me, as I collapsed in his arms. He lifted me up and carried me back to the couch, placing me down gently, as if I had been made of bone China. I guess I was just as breakable, if not more so. In fact, I felt as if I had already shattered into a million shards and only the shell was left to carry around the pieces.

"I am sorry, Emme," he said, stroking back my hair before leaving me alone, but just before he could shut the door behind him, I said,

"Boaz."

"Yes?"

"Can you tell him something for me." He nodded his head, telling me silently, that he would.

"Tell him that I'm sorry and that I hope... I hope he's happy with his Siren. That I will... *never forget him,*" I said, having to hold it together before this last part that was uttered as an agonizing whisper.

"I will pass on your message, little one," he told me with pity in his eyes.

*"Thank you... and... take care of yourself, Boaz,"* I said, making him bow to me before leaving and the second the door closed, my tears started all over again. Meaning that by the time they stopped, Roger was beyond pissed off at being made to wait.

It also meant that I didn't have my wits about me, and got swiped at, cutting another line down my hand. I swore and ran to the sink, cleaning it, and letting the blood run down the sink. But then, as I watched those ribbons of crimson merge with the water, flashes of memory started to come back to me.

"Gods, what is it?! Why can't I fucking remember?!" I shouted, slamming the tap down before covering my hand in a kitchen towel and slumping down to the floor, resting my head back against the fancy cupboards. The whole apartment was total luxury and was beyond anything I would have ever imagined for myself. It was all sleek lines and modern furniture, that wasn't me at all. But hey, at least I wasn't homeless while I looked for a new place to live. Because I knew there was no way that I could stay here.

I couldn't live in the pocket of the man I loved forever... *that was just plain wrong.* No, I had to find a way to move on. Not from my heartache, as I knew I never would, but I had to find a way to make something of a life for myself. Because despite what Kaiden thought, thanks to that video, I would never try to kill myself. Not even after losing him, which would have been the only thing to happen in my life that would have ever been a reason to.

But like I said, I would rather live in a world knowing he was happy, than not live in one just because he didn't choose me. Which was why I pulled myself off the floor and forced my body to work. To move through the motions of life. I started with a shower, letting my tears be washed away with the scent of my hospital stay. Because last night in the hospital came back to me, whereas his words made sense now.

He knew even then that he would be walking away from me.

*He knew it was goodbye.*

Ѱ

A week later, and each day was merging into the next. I didn't know how he knew, but the day after he walked away from me, I had a delivery…

*A new laptop.*

The only way he could have known was if Boaz had told him after noticing it smashed on the floor. Either way, the second I opened it, I found tears in my eyes as it seemed they weren't yet dried up like I had hoped. I wasn't sure why he did this but just knowing that he had thought of me only made it more painful. Because I knew it was from him, as the expensive tech wasn't all I received. No, a single piece of card had been with it.

One that was handwritten that said only one line…

*'For all your love stories.'*

It was both sweet as much as it was painful. Because I had no more happy stories to give the world. I had nothing left to believe in, for what was the point of finding love, only to have it ripped cruelly from your grasp. To give me a taste of the dream. The six-year dream that was now nothing but a bitter memory of loss.

And I had no one to blame but myself.

*I knew that.*

So, I carried on regardless, setting aside my new laptop and keeping it in its box, knowing that I would leave it here when I left. Something I had focused most of my time doing. Of course, in the envelope that had been left for me, had been credit cards with my name on them, along with bank cards that had pin numbers at the ready. But what I didn't have, was my own card and being in America, I had no idea how to get a new one sent to me. So, after a week of putting it off, I knew that I would have to ask someone in his life, thinking Hel might have been the best option.

Because I didn't want to use a penny of his money. Okay, so admittedly, I ate the food in the fridge until I got to a point that I knew I would need to go shopping soon. But without my own cards, then I was at a loss on what to do next.

I had rung the club numerous times before hanging up quickly. I had even been outside once just to check the bank cards, curious to know how much my 'promised care' had cost him.

When had seen how many zeros there were on the screen, I yelled out,

"What the Hell!?" I then looked around after likely scaring a few people, and said to random strangers,

"This is madness! Crazy... he can't do this!" Then I grabbed the card, snatching it from the machine before storming back to the apartment building as if I was on a mission. Although that mission pretty much consisted of pacing back and forth for thirty minutes while picking up the phone and hanging up again after only one ring. They must have thought they had a crazy person obsessed with Sins on their hands.

But I knew I would have to do something, because without my own money, I was never going to make it out of here and well, there were things like food that I needed to survive.

Meaning, there was no other option...

*I had to call him.*

# CHAPTER 22

# TORTURED SOULS
## WRATH

"Torturing yourself again, brother?" My brother's voice interrupted my daily routine, which admittedly these days was all centred around Emmeline...

My Lost Siren.

The one that got away. No, that's not right.

*The one I let go.*

I gritted my teeth bitterly, wondering if I would have fucking enamel left or would I grind it all off before my vessel had chance to produce more?

"I still don't understand it," I admitted for what felt like the same fucking argument I had with myself, along with my brother, ever since that day.

"Yes, so you keep saying," my brother responded dryly. Although, these days he was mostly pissed at me, so I wasn't to expect anything else. But then, I was fucking pissed at myself for fucking it all up so royally, so the self-loathing was nothing new. Because I'd been blessed enough to find my Siren and done everything wrong by her since. That was what it felt like. I had missed all the signs of her misery. But then, as my brother liked to remind me, I had kept her my prisoner and forced her to spend most of her time living here against her will. Was it any surprise she had felt desperate enough to find her own way out?

Gods, but how had I got it all so wrong?

I had foolishly believed that she loved me and all because of the way she had written me in that damn book! But none of it had been real. It had all be fiction. No doubt nothing more than an attraction on her part, for why else would she have pushed me so hard... pushed me towards another woman? Had she really even thought of her as my Siren, or had she just been a convenient way out?

No! I couldn't think of her that way. I couldn't sully the goodness in her nature with my bitter thoughts. No matter how much her drastic actions had hurt me. Gods, but just going back to finding out what had happened, I had nearly destroyed the whole fucking house, tearing apart the room we had shared in minutes.

In fact, had it not been for my brother, I would have lost myself to my Demon and never found my way back again. Just the fucking pain of watching that footage... *fuck*... but I had never cursed the Fates as much as I had that day. That was when I knew that I had no choice but to let her go. To give her what she truly wanted.

To let her believe I had found my Siren and it wasn't her.

Fucking lies!

Lies that had felt like fucking acid being poured down my throat, eating at my vessel's core from the inside out. The truth of it all had been me never setting eyes on Raina again and having my brother deal with her. Another life set up as compensation for her troubles in being brought here. But if she thought love was what she would find in me, then she had been foolishly mistaken.

For I loved only one.

*There would only ever be her.*

My lost Siren.

"What don't you get exactly?" my brother asked, referring back to my obsession… *Watching my girl*. Because as much as I knew it was wrong, I didn't fucking care. I had the whole apartment rigged with camaras, making the excuse that it was for her own safety. Of course, this hadn't been a total lie, but it also wasn't a whole truth either. Because had I not had this, I would have gone insane a week ago. My Demon would have taken over and nothing would have saved her from being taken and claimed. Something I couldn't ever allow to happen, not against her will. *I wouldn't do that to her.*

No, this was the lesser of two evils. So, I continued to watch her and violate her privacy. But there was one part of the footage I couldn't stop torturing myself with.

The day I left her.

Gods, but she had looked so broken. She had also looked so shocked at watching the footage, I knew then that she hadn't lied when she said that she hadn't remembered. I had watched her throw her laptop as agony and anger ripped through her, making me want to know why? It was the only part of this decision I had really struggled with when trying to convince myself that I was doing right by her.

Her reactions that day. The ones that mirrored my own heartbreak. Two tortured souls bound together, despite what she thought. Because there was no mistaking that she was my Siren, *there never had been.* In all honesty, I was now questioning why I had ever felt anything towards Raina, as since our time apart, I had lost all thoughts of her. Any slither of feelings I had foolishly thought there was, were now gone in an instant and that in itself had me questioning why?

"She was so hurt that day. Why, if her feelings towards me were nothing more than an author of my story feeling for her character, would she react in such a way?" Hel sighed after I said this, having his own very strong opinions on the matter. In fact, we had ended up punching it out more than once, ending the argument bloody and butting horns.

"You know my thoughts, brother, so I will not waste my time speaking them again." Needless to say, Hel hadn't agreed with my decision to let her go. But then, he hadn't been the one to pull her dying body out of the water and be forced to watch as the life drained out of her.

*The worst day of my existence.*

A memory that had fucked with my head as much as it had with my heart ever since. I woke roaring in agony most nights, calling her name like some fucking wounded beast howling for its mate. Gods, but I dreaded to think had I not got to her in time! Just watching her sleep for days on end had been torture enough.

I had tried to get my blood into her as quickly as I could, knowing that it would do little, but just enough so she would make it to the fucking hospital. After that, I took control of the doctor's minds, having my blood transferred into her intravenously just so her injuries would heal quicker. Then I wiped their minds of the injuries before they thought of her as some marvel of medical science.

Four fucking days!

But her body had been cut to ribbons from all the glass, with her head bleeding in my lap, making me fucking panic, biting into my hand over and over again trying to heal her quicker. But the one single injury on her that had bothered me the most was the one that I couldn't explain. The mark on her cheek, for I had been hit enough times in my life to know one when I saw it. That had not been an injury sustained from her fall.

Yet the footage told me all I needed to know, and all the things I didn't fucking want to see.

*She had jumped.*

"What is it, Lucy?" Hel's voice brought me back to the room, realising my brother was now on the phone. Then he grinned before turning my screen to face him, clicking on the pad a few times before nodding down at it, telling me to look for myself.

"Tell me when it happens again," he said, staying on the line and making me frown when I got to my feet so I could see what he was looking at. It was back to the live feed of her as she now paced up and down the living space with a cordless phone in her hand. She would look at it, then hit a button I was guessing was redial and hold it to her ear before ending it quickly.

"It just happened again, My Lord." I heard on the other end a girl named Lucy who worked behind the bar, and therefore was usually the one who answered the phone at the club.

"Of course, it did," my brother commented with a smirk, looking at me.

"Alright, leave it with us," he said before ending the call.

"She's calling the club then hanging up?" I asked, gathering as much but wanting it confirmed all the same.

"Looks like she is trying to get someone's attention," Hel replied with a knowing grin before asking,

"Question is, what are you going to do about it?"

I sighed at that, once promising myself that I would leave her alone. But then I also didn't count on her trying to reach out to me either. I growled low before grabbing my phone and internally saying, fuck it!

"About fucking time," my brother muttered, something I ignored as I listened to it ring, near laughing when I saw my girl scream and throw the phone onto the couch like it was a bomb about to go off. Then I watched as she paced some more, staring at it while talking to herself. I didn't know what she was saying as the video didn't have audio.

I think that would have pushed me over the edge, hearing her tears.

"Pick up, little Halo," I muttered, letting it ring until it rang off, something she prematurely relaxed about, letting her slim shoulders slump. But this lasted only seconds before I was ringing again, making her jump once more.

"She is a funny little thing," my brother commented, before she finally grabbed the phone, taking a second to compose herself by using a hand in the air as if this helped her take a deep breath, making Hel chuckle.

Then finally, my girl answered, and I was awarded with the sound of her voice once more.

"Hello?" I actually closed my eyes as emotions flooded me. Then needing to force my voice to sound steady, I answered her,

*"Hello, little Halo."*

# CHAPTER 23

# PUSHED INTO MY MEMORIES
## EMMELINE

"*Hello, Little Halo.*"

Gods, but just the sound of his voice had me falling back to the couch, putting a hand to my heart and needing a moment to stop it from pounding. Then I forced myself to say his name,

"*Kaiden.*" I swear I heard him fight back the urge to growl at this, and not in a bad way.

"Erm... what can I do for you?" I made myself ask, hoping to sound as calm as possible. After all, I didn't want to make this any harder for him.

"I would ask the same thing, as you're the one who has been ringing the club, sweetheart," he said in an amused tone, and not anything like the one I remembered the day he walked away. But him saying this also had me defensive in a heartbeat and my first instinct kicked in... *denial.*

"No... no, I haven't." At this he chuckled and called me on my bullshit with proof.

"We traced the number, Emmeline, so do you want to try

189

again? Only this time, by telling me why you keep calling," he said and again, it was a gentle reprimand, making me wonder why he was seemingly being so nice to me now. Did it have something to do with Raina? Was it because he was now happy? Fuck, but why was that so painful a thought, when all I wanted was him to be so?

"Okay fine, I called but I wasn't expecting to speak to you," I told him, now back tracking and he knew it.

"No? Then who were you hoping for?" he asked in a confident tone.

"Hel, I wanted to speak to Hel... is he... erm, there?" I asked, wincing and hitting myself silently on the side of the head. He chuckled for some reason before telling me,

"Yes, he is here and no, you can't speak to him."

"And why not?" I asked frowning at my coffee table.

"Because you can deal with me, now tell me what it is you need," he said sternly this time, and I sighed knowing that this was where the conversation was going to get difficult.

"Okay fine, I just need my bank cards back," I said, making him reply swiftly and surely.

"No."

"No?" I repeated, thinking this would help when it just made me sound dumb.

"I believe you are well acquainted with the concept, having heard it said from your lips many times." At this my mouth dropped open in shock, then I pulled the phone back so I could look down at it in disbelief like this would help because... *oh no he didn't just say that!*

"That's... I, erm, not... anyway... Look, I am not here to

make life difficult for you, quite the opposite actually," I said, sounding lame but making him question,

"How so?"

"Look, I just need my bank cards so I can... erm... start looking for my own place," I pushed out, making him actually laugh this time.

"Last time I checked, you have a place, just as you have bank cards."

"But none of it's mine," I told him, making him sigh this time.

"It is all yours, Emmeline." I started shaking my head again, not that he could see this.

"But I told you that I didn't want it... it's not mine... it's yours and it's not right," I tried to get my point across.

"There are many things that occurred between us that weren't right, Emmeline, but I can assure you that this is not one of them." Ouch, okay so that hurt.

"Please, I don't want to argue here," I told him.

"Excellent, for once we are on the same page," he commented arrogantly, making me grimace.

"That's not what I mean... well, I mean the not arguing bit but the money stuff we are definitely not on the same page. Hell, we are not even reading from the same book," I told him.

"And tell me, pretty girl, which book is that now... writing about me again?" he asked in a flirty tone that made me mouth, 'oh my god' before I had to clear my throat.

"Yes actually, it's called 'Wrath and the story of how he got his insanity back'. I know, I know, it's a bit wordy but I'm working on the title." At this he laughed, making me have to close my eyes at the sound, as it was another thing that shot straight to my heart... I missed his deep, gravelly laugh.

"Does it include how a curvy little curly blonde stole it from me?" he teased back, making me giggle and quickly ask myself if this conversation was actually happening. In fact, I nearly asked how Raina was, reminding him of the line he had already drawn between us, as this was messing with my head.

"No, but it might include the Mambo Number 5 as being your new favourite song." At this he was laughing again, and it made me bite my lip, trying to stop myself from grinning like a mad woman. Something I did regardless. But then my heart nearly stopped.

*"Missed my funny girl,"* he said suddenly, as if forgetting himself and making me suck in a quick breath. Had he really just said that?

*"Kaiden,"* I whispered his name, making him growl again.

"In answer to your question, no, you can't have your cards back and no, you can't move. Anything else you wish to do with your apartment and your money, is up to you," he said, getting serious again, making me shout,

"But you can't do that!" Of course this dispute was all in vain.

"I think you will find I can and have, in fact, already done just that," he replied calmly.

"Fine, then I will just use your money to get the next flight to England and go stay with a friend until I get myself sorted."

"Mmm, I think you will find you need a passport to do that, sweetheart, and wouldn't you know, I am looking at it right now." At this I gasped, not even thinking to look for the bloody thing!

"But... but... you... you can't do that!" I stammered out the same thing again, making the bastard actually chuckle this time.

"And once again, sweetheart, I already have."

"But why?! I don't understand why you would do this," I said throwing my hand up, a pointless gesture seeing as it was one he couldn't see.

"Because I want you exactly where you are," he admitted, making me inhale quickly again. Which was when I finally pushed it and said,

"But you have Raina, *you have your Siren.*" I added this last part on a painful whisper, making him growl down the phone and this time, it was not a gentle sound.

"What I have or do not have, is no longer your concern."

"But neither am I yours!" I countered back, making him snarl over the phone.

*"You will always be my concern, so don't push me into proving that to you!"* he shouted back, making me actually flinch before I didn't know what else to do other than suddenly hang up the phone. But then something he said suddenly assaulted me, and as I threw the phone to the side, I held my head in my hands. I ignored the way it rang back, doing so over and over again. No, now I was focusing instead on his words...

*Don't push me.*

"Fuck!" I shouted suddenly, knowing now the truth of

what happened that night as it came crashing back to me...
*back to my mind!*

Someone had tried to kill me.

I hadn't jumped after all.

No...

*I had been pushed.*

# CHAPTER 24
# CAUGHT

After this I yanked the cord out of the phone base just to get it to stop ringing constantly as it was clear that Kaiden was far from finished with our conversation. Half of me wanted to answer it and try once again to tell him what had really happened on the balcony that night.

But then, what was the point until I could find proof? I also had to ask myself, what did it even matter if he had already claimed Raina as his Siren? Although, what he had been doing still flirting with me down the phone, I had no idea. Or was it just this connection between us, would it forever be eternal, no matter what?

*Would we be forever connected?*

Well, no, because only one of us would live forever and it wasn't me. No, I would eventually die thinking about him still on my deathbed no doubt. I wondered if his name would be the last word spoken from my lips, as being the one and only man I had ever loved.

Which was why I needed him to know the truth. I

couldn't live with myself if I knew there was some way I could have told him. Could have proven to him once and for all that I hadn't jumped. That I hadn't been that desperate to get away from him. That I hadn't run from his love like he thought.

But like I said, half of me wondered what did it really matter? Then again, I had already spent far too long doubting myself when deep down I knew this was the right thing to do. I knew it wouldn't change anything between us but at the very least it might manage to bring closure to our story.

It might make the end bittersweet, instead of just bitter.

*The end.*

That was always a painful statement, whether it be written at the end of a story or spoken aloud to a loved one. Because no one wanted a good thing to end. Because unless you were eternal like Kaiden, then it was a reality you had to face. It was what made mortal life so precious, it could be over in an instant, as life was often fragile.

*The heart most definitely was.*

Which was why I did not want to look back on my life with anymore regret than I already had. Besides, Raina might have been his Siren but that didn't mean that I trusted her. In fact, after remembering what she had done, I outright hated the bitch! For once, there was no guilt that came with admitting it either, as she was the one that didn't deserve Kaiden. But unfortunately, there was no book written for the underserving Siren who was not worthy of their Enforcer. Who knows, after this, then maybe there would be.

But as for now, well it looked like there was only one way to make this happen, which meant only one thing…

*Another break-in.*

I jumped the moment there was a knock on the door, and before I could question who it was, a man shouted,

"It's just maintenance, Miss." I grinned at this as it didn't take a genius to know who had sent him up. So, I opened the door and let him in.

"We have had word your phoneline might be unplugged, I'm just here to check on that for you." I smirked and said,

"Help yourself, I have to go out anyway, so if you're cool to just let yourself out," I said, grabbing my jacket off the stand and stuffing my feet into a pair of running shoes. Then I couldn't help but smile to myself when the second he plugged it in, it started ringing. The maintenance man called out just as I was closing the door, to tell me about the phone no doubt. I called the lift and just as I was stepping inside, he opened the front door and told me what I already knew,

"Miss, it's Mr West on the phone, he really needs to speak with you."

"Tell him maybe another time, I'm just in such a rush getting a new passport," I said with a grin, already imagining Kaiden's angry face when he was told this. But then it served him right, trying to control my life like that. Still, it made me question why? Why, if he had moved on, was he not letting me do the same? Why did he want to keep me in New York so badly, when we were never to meet again?

It didn't make sense.

Well, one way or another, I was getting that proof and I was showing it to him, even if I had to email every person who worked at his club, he was going to see the truth...

*If it was the last thing I ever did.*

☿

Okay, so why I thought this was going to go any better than the first time, I had no clue! Oh yeah, because I didn't know that I was being followed from the moment I stepped out of the building or that Kaiden had Tristan acting as secret security guard since the very first day I was brought here.

*Kaiden had thought of everything.*

Which meant the second I'd got in a cab and made my way to Greenburgh, I was tailed. But more than that, as I got dropped off at the point I knew how to get in, seeing as it was the very same way I got out last time... *something they knew.*

So, after allowing myself to be led into a false sense of security, I snuck across the grounds, hence the running shoes and khaki parker jacket. One I had pulled tight thanks to the light rain that had started.

I was just hoping that they hadn't put a lock on the door or anything like that. But after making my way inside, this had been the least of my worries as the second I made it through to the other side, my troubles really began.

Oh, and it started with a voice I knew.

"Hey, doll face." I screamed at the sight of him leaning casually with his feet crossed and looking at his fingernails. But when he looked up at me and winked, I made my pointless attempt at running. As soon as I turned and tried to run, I was grabbed from behind, spun and tossed over another shoulder belonging to a Wrath Demon.

*"Fuck!"* I hissed, making him chuckle.

"Yeah, you got that right Doll, you're pretty much fucked."

"Okay, I can explain," I said after trying to struggle free

and getting nowhere... damn, but Hel was strong. It felt like an iron band held across my legs!

"Oh, I am sure, but before you do, go ahead and do me a favour and save it for my brother, because I have a feeling he is really not going to want to miss this." I sucked in a quick breath and said,

"Please don't do that."

"Not much I would keep from my brother, Doll, and you, well you're definitely not a secret I would risk my life on Earth for," he said, but we both knew that there was practically nothing Hel could have done to make his brother that killing mad.

After this, I stopped even trying to convince him, knowing there was no point. Which was why I just let him take me to what I gathered would be back to the room I knew. However, the moment we started to head down to the lowest levels of the mansion, I really started to panic.

"Wait, where are you taking me?!" I asked as we made our way down the cinder block hallway I remembered from my first time. Then he bent forwards and pulled my body down from his shoulder so I was now standing.

"Where do you think, the place we bring most prisoners."

"But I did nothing wrong," I argued.

"No?" he questioned, making me start walking backwards now there was that predatory look in his eyes.

"Because from where I'm standing, it looked like you just tried to break in to another building we own... question now is, why?" I started to shake my head, making him smirk.

"Oh, but don't worry, it's not me you need to tell, after

all…" he paused, walking me further backwards until I had nowhere to go but through the open door at my back. Then the moment I was clear, he shut the door to the cell and said though the window,

"It's been a while since my brother had someone cute to interrogate."


*Then he winked at me.*

# CHAPTER 25
# FULL CIRCLE
## WRATH

"Answer the fucking phone!" I roared after it rang on and on until it didn't. This was as I saw Emmeline yank the cord from the wall, cutting the connection, making me bellow,

"FUCK!" Then I rang the reception, making demands that they reconnect her phone in hopes she would see sense and pick up the fucking call this time. Because something had happened since I had said what I had, admittedly losing my temper when I promised myself that I wouldn't. But fuck, nobody pushed my buttons like she did, because I didn't fucking care enough about anyone but my brother.

But I could see something in her change.

Something had happened and I didn't know what. A fact that was sending me fucking crazy! Although, that wasn't the only thing that was messing with my head. No, because the very second she had said my name, I had felt my Demon relax for the first time since I last saw her. Fuck, but I had missed her voice. I had missed her quick wit and quirky humour. I had missed her little gasps and the way she got stuck for words around me. The way that even now, I knew I could still affect her.

But at its core, I had simply…

*Missed her.*

I watched the screen like it held sight of the Gods be damned elixir of life! Which for me, *I guess it did.* But then I frowned as she answered the door, letting a man in and making me growl, despite knowing he was just maintenance. He was there to fix her phoneline, something I waited for so I could ring the second it got connected. But then I narrowed my gaze on the screen.

"What are you doing now, little trouble maker?" I asked, snarling when I saw her stuffing her feet in her shoes and grabbing her jacket.

"Where do you think you are off to?" I questioned in irritation, ringing her number again, seeing the way she left just as the man answered.

"Stop Miss Raidne now and tell her Mr West needs to speak with her immediately!" I snapped, making him say,

"She has just left."

"Then I suggest you go catch up with her and get off the fucking phone," I snapped, making him mutter in agreement before leaving me to watch as he ran to the elevators. Thankfully the multiple cameras caught different angles along with every room in the apartment, like the sight of her now speaking to him from inside the elevator.

I was near shaking I was that furious when I saw the doors close with her still inside.

"Oh, you will pay for that one, little Siren," I warned on a growl, just before the man rushed inside to tell me what her reply to my demand had been.

"I am sorry, Mr West, but she told me to tell you that she was in a rush getting her new passport." I released an angry sigh and said,

*"Fine!"* Then I hung up and the next call I made was to who I had put on her security detail.

"She is on the move."

"Yeah, just clocked her, she's hailing a cab," Tristan said in a serious tone, as he was on the job and he never fucked around when he was working.

"Follow her, as I suspect she is not going where she claims she is."

"And where would that be?" he enquired.

"The British embassy." Tristan laughed at this before assuring me,

"I won't lose her."

"You had better not, or I will have your fucking head!" I barked, unable to help myself. Then I hung up, tossing my phone to the desk and dragging a hand down my face just as my brother smirked back at me, having heard everything. However, I could tell there was something else playing on his face, as if he knew something I didn't but wouldn't yet say.

"New passport, that was a nice touch," he commented, making me groan in frustration.

"I swear that little Halo will be what makes me go grey," I commented, running a hand over my tied hair and making my brother laugh.

"So, what will you do now?" he asked.

"Any ideas? I am open to suggestions."

"End this fucking charade and finally claim the girl?" he said.

"We have discussed this!" I snapped, making him sigh before getting up out of his chair and telling me,

"Fine, then do me a favour, save yourselves the pain and let me deal with her." I gritted my teeth at this, hating that he was fucking right and when I nearly told him to fuck off, he raised a brow at me.

"Fine! Just... just see the girl is safe and back in her apartment by nightfall." He nodded and told me,

"It will be done, trust me, I have a feeling her little adventure will not end the way she believes it will." I barely had it in me to respond to this, making him leave my office grinning.

But that had been nearly two hours ago, and I was getting fucking restless, for I hadn't heard a word. But then, I trusted my brother when he said he could deal with this and well, he hadn't once ever let me down. However, it was the not knowing that bothered me the most, despite knowing it was likely for the best. Nevertheless, before this point to ease my worries or the fragile state of my Demon, I had simply needed to turn on my computer screen to see her. To feed my obsession by drinking in the sight of her living her life. Yet now, staring at the empty apartment for so long was slowly driving me fucking insane!

Which was why I'd hit my limit, ringing my brother when I could no longer stand it.

"When you said you could handle this, I had hoped to hear something by now!" I snapped as he answered.

"She is fine, but I have been a little busy dealing with an intruder found breaking in," he snapped, making me growl.

"An intruder?!"

"A spy I suspect," he replied surprising me.

"You don't yet know?"

"I haven't yet had time to interrogate them, but hey, feel free to come down here and do it yourself, you most definitely seem in the mood for it," he commented dryly.

"Oh, I will gladly be there to break them," I said, cracking my knuckles on my left hand just by making a fist. I needed something to hurt, and Gods help them, that's all I would say.

"But what of my Siren?" I asked, getting to more important matters. *The most important.*

"Like I said, she is fine, now get your ass down here," Hel said, hanging up before I could ask more. But then if he had been dealing with this issue, could his mind be elsewhere, enough to let her slip through my net? Fuck, but I knew I should have dealt with the matter myself!

I was quickly out of my chair and making my way down to the lower levels, more intent on finding out exactly what had happened to her than bothering with this intruder. Which meant that by the time I got there and found my brother, I was already snapping at him,

"What do you mean she is fine!?" He smirked at this, and I swear I nearly punched him. However, the sneaky bastard nodded to the same interrogation room I had last been in when first coming across my Siren. A room I had forbidden anyone to enter since she left. It was my memory and my memory alone, not to be sullied by the spilling of enemy blood. But then he said,

"Why don't you have a look for yourself." I frowned in question before opening the door and finding the very last sight I ever expected to see.

My Siren once more in chains.

*"I believe you have an intruder to interrogate,"* he said, and the second I saw her suck in a deep breath, I finally allowed myself to grin. Before turning to him, squeezing his shoulder and telling him so she would most definitely hear.

"With pleasure, for I know…" I paused to look back at her before finishing my claim…

*"…I am going to enjoy this."*

# CHAPTER 26
## LIES AND CONFESSIONS
### EMMELINE

T he moment Kaiden appeared, I felt as if all the air was sucked from the room, making it suddenly difficult to breathe. It had only been a week since I saw him last, but I swear it felt like years for the impact the sight of him had on me. Because the moment that door opened and he saw me, his green eyes turned dark in seconds. Which meant that I hadn't been the only one affected by what was happening now.

Of course, I was no fool, as the moment Tristan had opened the cell and showed me the chains, I knew this was history repeating itself.

"You're enjoying this, aren't you?" I had asked him, making him give me one of those cocky grins.

"You bet, now we both know where running got you last time, so you gonna be good and let me put these on you, or do want me to get Hel in here to do it?" Tristan had asked, making me sigh before thrusting my arms forward.

"Good shout that, curly." I rolled my eyes and let him put me in chains before leading my busted ass into the same damn interrogation room for a second time. Then he offered me the same seat and locked my chains to the floor, finishing this recreation with a wink.

Which brought me to how I got into this mess, knowing that this time, I was going to need to come up with something a bit better than Mambo number five to get me out of this shit. Especially, when Kaiden told his brother that he was going to enjoy this before stepping inside and locking the door with nothing but a thought.

And like last time, the moment he started to come closer, I stood quickly, this time without knocking over the chair at least. However, Kaiden was obviously big on recreating this moment as well, and made the thing go skidding off to the side and out of his way.

"I can explain!" I ended up shouting quickly.

"Well, I have to say, my interrogation skills must have improved greatly if you are talking now at just the sight of me." He commented with a grin playing at his lips. And speaking of the sight of him, this time it was a dark-grey denim and a dark-red T-shirt that covered that abundance of muscles. A thick belt buckle separated the two, and today's choice looked like dark metal souls trying to escape Hell. It was very fitting for sure, given my current circumstances.

"I can explain."

"Oh I do hope so, but then again... I remember what happened last time when you didn't." I swallowed hard at this, knowing he was talking about my neck, which was when I quickly homed in on his own and stated in pure shock,

"You still let it scar?" At this his lips twitched again, as the handsome smile was there just waiting to break free.

"As I said I would," he replied and, I couldn't help but let his words soothe me. Although I had to stop myself from asking what his Siren would have thought about that.

"And your marks are gone, I see," he noted with a hard edge I would be a fool to ignore.

"Yeah, well I promise not to sing this time," I joked, trying to ease the tension like I always did when I was nervous.

"Pity," he said, making me swallow hard.

"Is it?" I asked stupidly, always pushing for more.

"Most definitely, for how will I get to punish you without your defiance?" he asked and this time, I sucked in a quick breath.

"I promise, I didn't come here to cause trouble," I said thinking this would help. But as he walked to my side of the table before leaning back against it, just like last time, he said,

"And yet, trouble is what you find yourself in… tell me, little Halo, why is that?" I released a deep sigh and told him,

"I came in search of something."

"And tell me, did you find it?" he asked, making me lift my shackled wrists and say,

"Not really my scene."

*"No, but it is mine,"* he growled low, and I knew it wasn't done in anger.

"Well, I think it's time you let me go," I suggested, and again, that grin just kept reappearing because, oh yeah, he was enjoying this. Now the question was… *why?*

"Oh, you do, do you?" he mocked.

"Yes, I do… look, come on, Kaiden, you know I am not your enemy… just let me go," I stated, shaking my shackled hands again and making the chains rattle between us.

"I did that once and have to say, sweetheart, it wasn't fun for me the first time." I swallowed hard hearing this, as I would have been a fool had his words not meant something to me.

"That was your decision," I reminded him rightly or wrongly.

"As it is now, so no, I am not letting you go again," he told me brazenly, making me frown in confusion.

"But why not?" I asked.

"Because you fucked up." He stated firmly, and I shook my head in question before trying to find the right words.

"How... how did... I fuck up?" I stammered out as he started to step closer and like history was on repeat, I started walking backwards until the chain was pulled taut. Then he ran his hand along the length of it by my hands, before gripping it in his fist. Then he snapped the links with the same amount of ease as last time. After this he yanked me to him and growled down at me,

*"You came back to me!"* I gasped in shock, and I swear, had my hair been down at this point, then I would have been blowing a lot more out of my eyes than just the few loose curls, as I looked up at him.

*"And there she is,"* he rumbled softly, and I couldn't help but realise, in that moment, that something deeper was going on here. No, this wasn't just Kaiden playing with a new victim, this was something more. This meant something to him by my being here now. Like I had flipped some switch that turned back time and had me facing the same Kaiden that I had done that first day in here. He was not the man that

had been standing by the windows trying to detach himself from the heartbreak of my reality. One where his words had cut straight through the bone. He was not the same man who walked away.

*Tried to walk away…* Until I had reeled him back in, and now the result of that was staring at a man that had hit his limit. That was how hard I had pushed by coming here.

"Now if memory serves me right, I never got to search you last time." His words stilled my thoughts but not my reactions, as I quickly tried to take a step away from him. This was something the chain held in his fist wouldn't allow, as I made it only a single step before he was preventing anything more to come between us.

"I don't have anything on me," I told him, making him look me up and down in that slow, predatory way, that once again, darkened his eyes for a dangerous second.

*"I see plenty,"* he stated firmly, before he raised a hand up to the camera and made a cutting motioning with his hand across his neck. My eyes shot to the corner and watched as the red light went out, making me inhale quickly. But as I was busy looking to the camera, I was taking my eyes of my captor, and that was a precarious game he was about to play. Because suddenly I found my back against the wall and my shackled hands held high above me.

"Kaiden!" I shouted his name in shock but the second he started to unzip my jacket, I held myself perfectly still with only my chest heaving as I tried to breathe through this. Because I knew that if he started touching me, then I would lose. I had tried so hard to get over the loss of his touch this last week. Tried to get over the memory of it, missing it more than I ever wanted to admit. Because admitting it

211

would make it real. It would give even more power to my heartbreak, and I wasn't sure how I could give it up again.

Which was why I pleaded,

*"Please... don't do this to me."* He growled low and told me,

"You do this to yourself when you brought temptation back here."

I gulped, and he didn't miss it or the way I sucked air through barely closed teeth when his free hand snaked across my belly. A slow, sensual motion that purposely lifted up the material of my top as if he were desperate to feel my skin once more.

"Now what will I find, I wonder?" he asked, making me tell him,

"I was caught before I could find anything."

"But you were looking for something. Tell me, pretty girl, what was it you were hoping to find?" he asked in a calm and seductive tone I knew not to trust. Because that was the danger of Kaiden, he could turn heated in a heartbeat.

"Not this," I answered with honesty, making him scoff.

"Yet here we are... now the question is, where do we go from this point I wonder?" I shook my head a little and said in what I knew was a small voice,

*"I don't know."* He stilled his hand a moment as if my words affected him, before he continued on with the journey of rediscovering my body.

"Then let's find out, should we?" His rumbled reply shocked me as his head dipped and he forced my arms over his head, literally shackling me to him.

"Wh...what... are you... doing?" I stammered out as he

lifted my body up the length of him, giving me no choice in the matter.

"I think that's obvious, little one," he told me, hoisting me up so as our faces were level, and I could barely breathe being this close... close enough to feel his heart beating against my own heaving chest.

*"We shouldn't be doing this,"* I told him on a desperate whisper, when half of me was screaming to shut up and let him do whatever it was he wanted to do to me. Just so long as I remained locked to him in his arms.

*"We... should have never of been apart,"* he growled back, emphasizing the word 'we' and causing me to go stilled in his arms.

"But... but... you can't mean that... you..."

His hold tightened on me in response before a hand found its way to my ass, gripping me tighter to him as it freed up his other hand to make its way to my hair. Then with his fingers fisting a handful full of curls, he used this hold on me to force my head to the side. This was so as he had more room to bury his face in my neck, now breathing me in deep, as if I was an addiction he had been far too long without.

*"I mean every word,"* he told me and again, I was fighting for air enough to say the very last thing that I wanted to. But it was also the one thing that I knew I had to.

"And what about Raina? *What about your Siren?"* I felt him go tense and growl into my neck, before pulling back and telling me,

*"I hold my Siren in my arms right now."*

The second he said this, I cried out, feeling tears coating my eyes as my emotions bubbled over, and he didn't miss it.

Yet despite my fears, my pain, my heartbreak, I had to force out the obvious, despite knowing it had the power to crush my dreams once and for all.

But then again, with a single answer, it also had the power to ignite them once more.

"But… but you told me… *you claimed Raina as your Siren.*" He growled at this, and before his lips took my own, he whispered the truth over them, making me cry out at his admission…

*"I lied."*

## CHAPTER 27
# ROOTS OF OBSESSION

I cried out the second he said this, and it was a sound that was swallowed up whole by his kiss. One that I had no power to fight against as I craved it as much as he did. Because I would have been a fool to think differently, as his actions spoke louder than his words. Words that already had held such power over me. This meant that his touch utterly consumed me and rendered me defenceless against what was happening now.

The kiss was our most passionate yet, and after a week of being starved of each other's touch, then I couldn't be surprised. But despite this, I also knew there was that nagging voice in the back of my head that was screaming out the fact that he had lied. That he had put us both through this agony and I needed to get to the bottom of why. Why had he lied about Raina being his Siren?

And more importantly, *where was she now?*

"No, we have to stop," I said when the voice got too loud to ignore anymore, and this time it sounded like it was his Demon snarling.

*"Never!"*

I gasped in shock and again it was a sound drowned out by his kiss. One he deepened even further, as I swear he was trying to burn me up inside as I clung onto his neck, instead of trying to push him away. But then the moment I was gasping for air, he knew I had hit my limit. Which also meant that his concern for me overrode his need, and he pulled back enough to place his forehead to mine as we took deep breaths together. I started shaking my head a little, whispering,

*"Please, Kaiden... I don't understand what's happening here."* At this he sighed and told me,

"Don't fight it, Emmeline, for I let you go once, but I refuse to do it again, not when it was you that... *came back to me."* I frowned at his words and pulled back enough so as I could look at him.

"But how could you lie to me like that... *how could you break my heart?"* I whispered this last part, and his body went rock solid next to my own. Then he asked in a dangerous tone,

*"What did you say?"* I lifted my arms up from his head and asked,

"Please put me down?"

"No! Now answer my question!" he snapped, making me shout,

"I will if you put me down!" Suddenly my feet found the floor, but this didn't mean I was in any better position as he was now towering over me, back against a wall.

"Now, repeat what you said!" he demanded quickly.

"Why, so you can hear how much you hurt me by

walking away?" I threw at him as I tried to get away, and making his hands fist in my jacket, holding me still.

"I did what you wanted me to do!" he shouted back.

"And who told you that? It certainly wasn't me!" I snapped in return, and he pushed off the wall from me angrily, dragging a hand over his hair.

"Your actions are what told me that," he replied in an angry yet pained way. Which was when I lost my shit, and I stepped right up to him, despite him being huge compared to me. He turned just in time for me to push him, shocking the shit out of him enough that he went back a step.

"I didn't try and kill myself!" At this he closed his eyes and answered me in a strained voice,

*"I saw you."* This just managed to make my anger mount to even greater heights.

"I don't give a shit what you saw! I know the truth... I remember it now, and that was what I came here to find," I told him in a firm tone.

"What did you come to find?" he asked, raising a brow, so I told him the truth.

"I came here to find proof."

"And what were you hoping to achieve with it?" was his next question, and I released a frustrated sigh, throwing my hands up in the air dramatically.

"What do you think, you big idiot? I came here to prove it *to you!*" I snapped, poking him in the chest this time, making him look down at the action in shock.

"You came here to prove to me that you didn't jump?" he asked as if needing to establish this fully.

"That's what I am trying to tell you! Gods, what is it

with… Ah!" I ended this the second I was picked up and put on the table, a cry that ended up finishing with a moan of pleasure as he was suddenly kissing me again. And in between this kiss, he pulled back to speak.

"You didn't want me to leave you?" Again, his kiss didn't wait for an answer, only when I pulled back and said,

"No, you idiot." Then I grabbed him roughly so as to kiss him back, making him growl.

*"You said that already,"* he stopped to say, referring to me calling him an idiot.

"Good, then maybe you will listen," I said before going for his neck, kissing him there this time and making him groan as I headed for the scar I had made, licking up its length.

"You really didn't jump?" he asked again, making me bite down, and he growled before I let go and placed both my hands on his face, telling him sincerely this time,

*"No, Kaiden, I didn't jump."* At this he kissed me again, stopping only long enough to admit,

"Then I am an idiot." I giggled at that, doing so over his lips.

"Yeah, but what you gonna do? *Because you're my idiot,"* I told him, making him growl and his hands fisted in my jacket before demanding,

*"Say that again."*

"I think we have established the extent of your idiocy," I commented dryly, making him snarl,

"You know what I want, *so don't play with me, girl!"*

"Fine! You're mine, you big ape!" I shouted, before hooking my chained hands over his head, grabbing his hair and dragging his lips back to mine, and this time, I was the one to swallow his sounds. A cocky reply that ended up with me finding myself on my back with Kaiden firmly on top of me.

*"Too fucking right, I am!"* he snarled, making me moan even louder and this time, it wasn't just from his possessive kiss, but from the growl of his claim.

*He was mine.*

"About fucking time!" I told him back, wrapping my legs around him and grinding myself against his straining cock.

"Don't make me claim my Siren on a fucking table!" he snapped, and I pushed myself up purposely, telling him,

"Why not? This is after all, *our room.*" After this, he lost it, as every single restraint snapped, including my chains. Finally, my hands were free with only the cuffs remaining. Which meant that I was free to touch him as I pleased. He threw his head back and growled as I raked my nails over his back, dragging his T-shirt up and trying to get it off him as quickly as possible... *something that wasn't fucking working.*

"I can't take your virginity on a fucking table," he told me, making me reach up, take hold of the back of his neck and pull him closer so as I could whisper over his lips,

*"Don't be a pussy."* Then I kissed him, making him snarl and grip me tighter.

"You deserve better... *My Siren deserves everything."*

*"Then give me everything, handsome,"* I told him on a moan and to this, he picked me up, fully intent on doing just that. He unlocked the room and was carrying me out with

haste. Doing so now with me wrapped around him, but this put me at the angle to see straight into the surveillance room. Which had me quickly stopping him.

"No, wait!"

"No, for I have fucking waited long enough!" he snapped, making me tap him on the back of the neck. A spot I knew got through to him.

"Please, just give me a minute, I need to see... *I need to know, Kaiden,*" I told him, nodding to the room so he could see what it was I was referring to.

"I don't want this hanging between us... *I don't want anything standing between us anymore,*" I said again, and something in my eyes must have told him how much I needed this as he nodded. Then he let my legs go so I could walk into that room, one that was empty at his request no doubt.

So, I entered the room full of monitors, all holding pictures of every room in the mansion, other than Kaiden's suite along with Hel's. Their private space was kept private. But as I approached the monitors, Kaiden stepped up to my back and told me,

"Then if you want nothing between us, there is something I must show you." I couldn't help but hold myself tense at this, bracing myself for more of his confessions. Something that started when he reached around me. At the same time, he wrapped his arm around my waist as if he feared I would try running from him the second he showed me. Meaning that the moment he pressed a few keys on the keyboard, I was left so shocked I sucked in a startled breath, one that was lost to the sight in front of me.

*"What...what is this?"* I asked breathlessly, as I saw every inch of what had been my apartment for a short while, one now displayed on multiple screens. Then he pulled me back tighter against him and whispered in my ear,

*"The root of my obsession."* My mouth opened on a gasp, knowing that he had been watching me all this time.

"You didn't walk away?" I braved to ask.

*"Never,"* he told me, and I felt the tears start to blur my vision.

*"You didn't get over me?"* I asked on a shaky breath, and again his arm tightened around me before he whispered firmly,

*"There is no getting over your Siren, Emmeline."* At this I could stand it no longer as I turned in his arms and as my tears overflowed, I threw my arms around him, shouting his name,

"Oh Kaiden!" Then I cried in his arms, and he let me, holding me to him knowing that I needed this. I needed this moment between us. I needed it to heal.

*We both did.*

But this wasn't all I needed as I pulled back enough so as I could tell him the most important thing. The real reason I was here. The words I wanted to say the most.

"I should have told you this long ago… wanted to the moment you first kissed me. These feelings I have… Gods, but I wanted to tell you so many times…"

"Emmeline, you just need to tell…" I quickly covered his mouth,

"I love you," I interrupted quickly, feeling as if it would burst from me if I didn't, and he froze solid the second the

221

words were out. But then I was in his arms and my ass landed on the desk before my face was captured in his hands.

*"You love me?"* he asked me, tenderly wiping the tears from under my eyes with his thumbs, as if needing to hear it confirmed once more.

"I do. *I always have, Kaiden,"* I told him, making him close his eyes for a second and when he opened them, I saw something I never have before. Something I never ever expected to see on him.

*Tears.*

His own tears shimmered over green depths. Then he told me fervently,

"I have loved you since first stepping foot in that interrogation room, seeing my little Halo for the first time," he said, referring not only to me but to the hair he now reached up and played with, making me sigh happily at this, and I whispered his name,

*"Oh Kaiden."* This time when he kissed me it was one that poured every ounce of emotion and love into it. It was his tenderness that had even more tears falling as I felt his love, his obsession, his caring heart. I felt it all in a single kiss. But then the moment between us was broken as my hand rested back against the desk, hitting something on the keyboard that activated something new.

Suddenly my panicked voice was heard.

'Let me go!' Kaiden froze and I quickly said,

"I didn't say that." And we both turned our heads to look at the screens, and I gasped the second I saw what actually had happened that night now playing on the monitor. It was me trying desperately to fight myself free of the person that had me in their grasp, soon trying to force my body over the balcony. Kaiden growled angrily as he reached out and gripped the screen in his large hand, and I heard it start to tear from the mount on the wall.

'NO, STOP THIS!' I screamed on the video, and I winced, having no choice but to force myself through the nightmare of that night all over again. But then as soon as I was finally pushed, the screen cracked as Kaiden crushed the side in his now Demonic hand.

*"You were pushed!"* he snarled in the depth of his fury and as he turned to me, more of his Demon was looking back at me than the face I was used to. However, I didn't even flinch this time but instead confirmed,

"I was pushed." At this he ripped the screen from the wall, making me jump as he threw it down on the floor, and before a single piece even touched me, he had me covered in his arms. He then buried his head in my neck, telling me in a gravelly Demonic voice that was the first time I had ever heard it full of emotion,

*"We didn't believe you... you tried to tell us, and we didn't believe you."* This came not only from the man I loved, but from the Demon in him as well.

"It's okay," I told them both, making him hold me tighter, being careful enough to keep his claws from my skin.

*"It is anything but!"* he told me sternly, and the moment he pulled back, he cupped my cheek in his Demonic hand.

"I almost lost you... *I let you go."* This time it was Kaiden's voice and I swear, the sound of it breaking at the end made my heart ache for him.

"But that's the thing about love, if it's strong enough, it will always come back to you, especially if it belongs to you… which I do, *seeing as… I am your Siren,"* I said, admitting this for the first time.

It had the affect I knew it would as suddenly, Kaiden crushed his lips to my own, snarling the only two words he now needed to say…

*"My Siren!"*

# CHAPTER 28
# CLAIMING HALO'S
## WRATH

Fuck! But the moment I heard these words, I was both a man and Demon lost. Lost to the perfection in both her claim and the sight of my Siren. The tears that clung to her glistening eyes, granting me a window into her soul and showing me the love she held for me there.

It was the closest I would ever come to experiencing my personal Heaven.

Although I wasn't entirely sure this was true, as I had a feeling finally claiming her was going to grant me that. Speaking of which, that was precisely what I was going to do right now, and like I said to her, *it wouldn't be on some fucking table!* For I had done so much wrong by her, it was time I start doing right. Which was why I picked her up in my arms and left the room, leaving the agony of truth behind us. Because she hadn't jumped. Just like she claimed. Just like she said she never could.

*I should have believed her.*

I should have damned whatever I saw on that screen and believed my Siren above all else. I should have trusted her!

225

Well, I would not fail her now. I would not tarnish our love with distrust ever again. Because she had never tried to leave me like I feared she had.

*No, someone had tried to fucking take her from me!*

Blood would be spilled, and death would happen this very night. But as for right now, there was something far more important than my vengeance, far more important than my Wrath. And like I said, I would not fail her again. I would not put this need for revenge before her, for nothing could stop this. Nothing could stop me from finally claiming my Siren.

Not now we both had made the claim.

Which was why I carried her through the mansion, holding to me the most precious gift from the Gods, eager to get to what would soon be forever known as the heart of our home.

The bed I would finally have her in.

*Our bed.*

I could tell she knew this when she didn't fret as I walked us both inside my room. She no longer looked around with fear in her eyes, and there were no longer any words trying to convince me that she didn't belong here. She was the only one that would ever fucking belong here! For she was mine and now, it was time to make it everlasting. Which was why I carried her up to my bed, but instead of laying her down on it, I let her feet find the floor.

Fuck me, but the way those big eyes looked up at me now, made me feel like a fucking God looking down at his Goddess. It was why I caressed the back of my fingers down her cheek with a tenderness I felt down to my very core… *down to the very heart of me.*

"You are so beautiful, you make me ache for you," I told her, allowing my emotion to coat my words in honesty. Her eyes closed as she bit her lip, before whispering a shy, little,

*"Thank you."* Then because she wanted me to have a piece of her thoughts, she added quickly,

"You're very handsome too."

I couldn't help but chuckle at this, as she was so endearing, I just wanted to scoop her up and hold her in my arms forever. However, this wasn't all I wanted to do to her, which was why I started to gently slip her jacket from her shoulders, making her shudder at my touch.

I knew then that she was nervous, for I heard her heart flutter, speeding up its already erratic beat. Her pulse increased and her breaths caught the moment I then reached for the T-shirt she wore. Then without stopping, I pulled it up over her head, no longer trying to tear her clothes from her body but instead savouring every moment of this.

I wanted every second of it immortalized in my mind so as I could think of it often. So as I could treasure the moment I finally claimed the only thing in my life I ever wanted. My gorgeous Halo.

*My Emmeline.*

Because it wasn't solely my Siren I was in love with, but the girl who was standing before me now, looking so nervous. The cutest girl in the whole fucking world and yet, the only one bold enough to take on my Demon. To take on one of the most feared Demons in all of Hell and yet, we were both putty in her hands for her to mould us into whatever she saw fit. We were both a slave to her and she had not one fucking clue!

*Well, that was about to change.*

Starting with getting her out of the rest of her clothes.

*"Kaiden, I..."* she whispered ever so quietly as I tugged open her jeans, needing to see the rest of her.

"Yes, little Halo... what is it you need?" I questioned, and I swear my voice sounded out of the depths of normality, as I purred each word.

*"I only need you,"* she admitted, and I growled before grabbing her, lifting her off her feet and making her fall back to the bed, igniting little gasps from her at my sudden actions. But then, how could I stop when she spoke like that? Telling me so sweetly that it was I that was all she needed? The only words I had longed to hear.

*Well, not the only ones.*

"Tell me who it is you belong to?" I demanded of her, for I was a bastard lost to the idea of owning her... *every delectable inch of her!*

"Kaiden, I..."

"Tell me!" I insisted again, letting my growl strengthen my demand as I started to remove her shoes and socks.

"You, *I belong to you."* She gave me what I wanted... what I needed, making me growl over her lips,

"Yes, you fucking do!" Then I kissed her, fucking addicted to the taste of her! But this was no longer enough as my need for her was riding me even harder than ever before. Which was why I left the comfort of her arms and the splendour of her lips, so as I could stand before her, then taking hold of her waist band, I warned her,

"Tell me now, Emmeline, tell me to stop if you are not yet ready for this," I said, needing to give her at least one chance at taking this slow. For I knew this was her first time and fuck me, but if that thought didn't have my heart racing and my mouth watering. My Demon was practically roaring in my head, telling me to shut the fuck up!

*"I... want this... I want you,"* she told me shyly, and that was where my restraint snapped and fucked off, never to be seen again. My reply came in the form of action as I tore her jeans down her legs, making her gasp.

I swear, just the sight of her in nothing but black lace had me trying to hold back my Wrath. Because I wanted to take her as a man first, knowing that he would eventually get his chance at her. But for now, this was my time.

It was our time... *mine and Emmeline's.*

So, I tore my own clothes from my body, the sound from my boots echoing in the room. I fucking loved the way she drank in the sight, as she always did. I swear I felt like a fucking peacock, wanting to tense my muscles just so as she would grant me that lustful wide-eyed look. I fucking adored those eyes of hers. And all that creamy skin but Gods, her hair, I needed to see it spread out around her head against my sheets, which was why I told her,

"Take down your hair." Not the first time I had demanded as much. But being the perfection she was, the perfect little submissive, she reached up and did as I asked, causing me to force myself not to put a fist to my fucking mouth to stop me from groaning. I had never seen a more beautiful sight in all my life!

*She was my everything.*

Now it was time to make her mine in every way. I lowered myself slowly over her, crawling my way up her body like I wanted to fucking devour her, something, admittedly, I did. But then her delicate little hands touched me, and I couldn't stop the groan this time, as I fucking loved her touch. The way she followed the lines of my muscles, as if memorizing the map of my body.

Soon I would have her thinking of little else.

For it was time…

*To make my Siren sing only my name this time.*

# CHAPTER 29
# WHERE DID MY HEART GO?
## EMMELINE

He started crawling his large, muscular body over me, and I was nearly panting by the time he reached my lips. He was completely naked and for once, I had not shied away from drinking in my fill. I wanted to trace every painted line with my fingertips, taking the time to explore every tattooed picture over his skin. I wanted to know the meaning of them all, the stories he had to tell from his own lips. I just knew that I would hang on every single word.

But as for now, well it wasn't the time for words.

*It was the time for something else.*

To say that I wasn't nervous would have been a lie and I think he knew it, as he caressed a hand back over my hair. Then he lowered himself over me and whispered in my ear,

*"Relax, little one, I will take good care of you."* I released a breath at the sexual growl of his words, knowing this could be taken in so many ways and all of them good. But then he started to kiss my neck and I couldn't help but

moan, arching my back up, pressing my breasts against his chest and making him chuckle.

"So responsive to my touch, as it should be."

"Then I would do it some more... *just to be sure.*" I braved to tease him, making him smirk down at me before he told me,

"Always as my Siren wishes." Then he started to kiss his way down my body, but this was when I noticed his hand started to change as the rest of him remained the same. His Demon was coming through and more than that... *he was letting him.*

*"Kaiden?"* I said his name in a fearful question, making him coo down at me,

"Hush now, don't fear me... *Don't ever fear us.*" Then he used one of his talons to cut down the centre of my bra, making it snap open. My breasts burst free, ready for his touch, but he didn't stop there. No, because I felt the back of his talon caress dangerously down my belly, its smoothness luring me into trusting its touch. Which was why I gasped the second the tip hooked the waistband of my lacy briefs, and without any resistance, it cut through the material as easy as a knife sliding through paper.

Then when not an inch of my body was confined, no longer hidden from him, he grinned down at me, and on another sexual growl, told me,

*"Fucking perfection."* Then he continued with his kisses, until his lips were at my core, spreading my legs wide and tasting me. I swear I nearly shot off the bed as my shoulders pressed into the sheets and my back arched. However, his Demonic hand reached up and positioned itself at my belly, pressing me down with ease. The strength of his hold had me

flat in seconds, and was not something I had any chance at fighting against. Not even in response to what his tongue was now doing to my core. He tasted me so deeply, I blushed crimson as he speared the entrance before drinking back my arousal. Then he licked his way up my seam and latched onto my clit, making me fight harder against his dominate hold.

I was surprised that his claws didn't penetrate the skin, as they tapped against me in warning every time I tried to rear up from the bed. Naturally, it didn't take long before I was screaming out my release, this time screaming his name just like he wanted.

"Kaiden!"

At this, he bit down, making my release shoot up another notch, making me bellow,

"KAIDEN!"

He chuckled at this, soothing the string of his assault as I panted through the end of my orgasm.

"That's better," he stated, referring to me screaming louder for him. Then he kissed my clit once more, making me shudder before he rose up, and even in the euphoria of my release, I knew what came next.

"Offer yourself to me, Emmeline, you know what to do," he told me in a hard tone that spoke of his own arousal. But that wasn't all it spoke of, as it told me how desperate and on edge he was just to have me. But of course, I knew what he meant as I had written it, and it was one scene where I'd secretly only had myself in mind when putting the words down.

*He wanted me to submit.*

So, I did as my Enforcer wanted, letting my legs fall

233

open even wider, and turned my head to the side offering him my neck. He rumbled a growl of pleasure at this, before positioning his hard cock at my core, at the same time lowering his lips to my awaiting skin. Then he told me,

"This will only hurt for a moment… *but it will hurt so sweetly, I promise."* Then before I could worry more, he thrust his entire length up inside me, at the same time biting my neck and piercing his Demonic fangs through my flesh. I screamed at the pain he spoke of, but before I could try and squirm free of him, he reached up and held my head in position with a fist in my hair at the top of my head. Then he moved his cock again at the same time sucking back my blood, which was when my entire world started to tilt on its axis.

*I came like never before!*

"KAIDEN! AHHH YES!" I roared as the strongest, most powerful orgasm of my life tore through me, feeling as if it had the strength to shatter me. But Kaiden had me held tightly in his arms, not letting me go anywhere as my whole body trembled in his hold.

"Beautiful. Hell… so fucking beautiful," he told me, referring me to his home and his own version of Heaven. But this growled admission was quickly followed by snarling down at me with lips bloody, and long fangs dripping crimson.

*"I want more… give me more!"*

Then he went back to drinking me down while moving inside of me, and now there was no sweet pain like he said there would be, there was nothing but sweet pleasure.

*"Yesss!"* I cried out as I felt it start to build once more, and this time it wasn't suddenly tearing through me, but

caressing my body with its slow burn. But then he started to move faster, harder, growling when he forced himself to slow, thinking I had hit my limit.

"I don't want to hurt you," he admitted, making me raise a hand to his face as I told him,

"Fuck me, love me, make me yours the way you need to... *the way we both need you to.*"

At this he growled low, which was my only reply as he took my words as permission for him to do with me as he wanted. And fuck me, if that thought didn't make me come screaming seconds after he started to hammer into me with untamed pleasure! His hands pinning me down by my still shackled wrists, holding me still for his body to claim me the way he needed to. *The way I craved for him to.* Because I was his Siren, and I wanted to take every brutal inch of love he gave me!

*And I did.*

I came screaming once more, at the very same time as he threw his head back and roared at the ceiling, actually making the walls crack with the force of his release. I felt his hard cock pumping inside of me as it emptied his balls of his seed. There was so much cum I could feel it bursting out of me around the base of his erection, one buried to the hilt, making me claw at the sheets beneath me. My insides were still quivering around the length of him as the aftershocks of my release fluttered like mini orgasms, making him harden still.

"Gods, but *I love you, my Emmeline,*" he whispered down at me, now kissing my jaw and my cheek before getting to my lips. A pair open and ready for him as I was still panting and gasping from the most amazing experience of my life, with the hope of many more to come after it.

"Are you okay, I was too rough with you?" he asked, the fear that he had hurt me was clear to see.

"No, you... it... *was perfect.*" His reply to this was to gather me up in his arms and hold me tightly to his body, using his elbows on the bed to keep most of his weight off me. But the secure, warm hold made me feel treasured, just the same as when he was whispering my name against my neck,

*"My sweet Emmeline, I..."*

His whisper of words was suddenly cut off, along with his weight.

*Along with his body.*

And I opened my eyes in shock to find the very last thing I ever expected to...

*Kaiden was gone.*

# CHAPTER 30
## MISSING BROTHER

"Hell!" I shouted as soon as I opened the door in my panic to find someone to help. Because the moment I realised Kaiden had disappeared, I had bolted up right. Then after looking down at myself, I realised that I was a mess, *a sexual mess*. I had his cum dripping out of me, combined with the blood of my virginity, and blood still down my neck and breast. I reached up and touched my bite, feeling nothing there but the blood he had missed to consume. But as for any tears in my skin, there was none, as he must have healed me as soon as he removed his fangs from my flesh.

But none of this was important now, as I needed to find the man who had just claimed me. My Demon Enforcer. Which was why I grabbed his T-shirt from the floor, and cleaned myself the best I could. This before grabbing my own clothes, the ones that had survived that was, and dressed quickly. I had no bra and no knickers, but I didn't care, I yanked on my jeans and my T-shirt before grabbing my jacket. I kicked my feet into my shoes and ran towards the door, opening it to find Hel standing there, seconds away from bursting inside.

"Emmeline!" he shouted my name before grabbing my hand and telling me,

"I have to get you out of here!" I shook my head, not understanding and pulling back a little, or at least trying to.

"Why, what happened, where is Kaiden? He just disappeared!" I told him in a rush.

*"I know,"* he gritted out. Which was when I snatched my hand from his and demanded,

"What's going on?!"

"Hell felt one of the Princes of Wrath claiming his Siren."

I started to shake my head in confusion, hating the pit in my stomach his words created.

*"I... I don't understand?"* I told him in a quiet voice.

"He is in Hell, Emmeline!" he snapped, making me gasp, covering my mouth with shaky hands.

*"No... but... how... why?"*

"Our father, he is not pleased... Look, just trust me, okay? I have to get you out of here... I have to get you somewhere safe!" he said quickly, making me nod, now running with my hand back in his. My head was a mess as I felt nothing but guilt at what had happened... all because of me. But none of it made sense. I had never written his father being displeased with one of his sons claiming his Siren, so I didn't understand, why now? Why me? But then, just because I had written it, didn't make it an absolute, as look at Raina. Speaking of which, where was she? Why hadn't I thought to ask that until now? Oh yeah, because I was too busy getting a Wrath Demon into trouble with his dad!

"Where are we going?" I asked when we got outside the house, seeing there was now a car waiting.

"I know a place, somewhere only I and my brother know about," he told me, and I frowned back at him.

"Wait, did he know this could happen?" I questioned painfully.

"He suspected that it might, so we had this plan as a backup," Hel said in a strained voice.

"But what will happen to him now?" He could see my panic mounting by the second.

"I don't know... Look, it will be okay, I just need to get you somewhere safe and then we will go from there."

"I don't give a shit about me! I just need you to save Kaiden!" I snapped, worried out of my mind!

"And he would only want you safe. Please, Emmeline, don't make this any harder... just get in the fucking car, okay?" I nodded after this and did as he asked, looking back at the house, unable to help the anxious tears from falling.

But then as we drove away, I didn't only have Kaiden's future to question, but also...

*Where were all the guards?*

# CHAPTER 31
# FATHERLY ADVICE
## WRATH

*ucking Hell!*

I roared in untamed fury as I felt my body being ripped from hers, finding my Demonic form now standing in the hallowing fields of destitute. It was where desperate souls roamed lost and screaming through the endless, long, black grass. It also boarded our lands, as this was the outskirts of Greed. Hence why all those stripped of what they held dear and more precious to them than the lives of others, now walked without purpose. They ambled through this world, chained to this prison without locks or bars, searching for gold, power, and anything else they had once killed for.

But in my anger, my Demonic arm lashed out at the nearest soul, nothing more than a withering skeletal figure and mere ghost of the vessel it once was. It shattered on impact, flying backwards, its pieces disappearing in the grass that moved like gentle waves of a black sea. It wouldn't die, for that was too much mercy for punishment. No, it would simply take years to find its pieces again and spend its days having no choice but to put itself back together.

Not that I gave a fuck, I was a Prince of Hell for fucks sake! I wasn't born to this land to make it easy on the sinful. The other side of our land of Anger and Wrath, was Heresy, for those souls that acted against the Gods and were punished for it. Neither place I needed to be right now, making me roar,

"SHOW YOURSELF, FATHER!" At this I heard his sadistic laugh before he appeared behind me, making me snarl,

"Why did you summon me?!" I snapped, knowing it was him as he was the only one that ever could, connected by our shared blood.

"Is that any way to greet your old man?" he said, making me sneer despite liking the bastard.

"You are no man," I told him, despite how he looked. But his vessel was similar to mine in size, not being one to allow his sons to best him in looks. His face however, was all hard lines, tanned skin, and dark eyes that were ringed with the same blue as my brother's. His lips always curled in a knowing grin, also reminding me of Hel's. I also knew that by today's standards of what was considered handsome in a rough-cut type of way, then my father would have been classed as such.

"But I do so enjoy this vessel and so do those in the house of Lust."

I scoffed at this, knowing of his friendship with the King of that particular sexually deviant realm.

"I have just fucking claimed…!"

"Your Siren, yes, I know… congratulations by the way, to think, one of my sons blessed with one from the Heavens… *I am so proud,"* he said in jest, making me scoff,

"Great, send me fucking dead flowers next time, would you? Not rip me from my Siren's dripping core after I just spilled my seed."

"Mmm, a good fuck, was she?" he asked, making me suddenly grab my father by the throat and squeeze. What not many knew was that I could best my father in this form, being stronger than him in my realm.

"Easy, Kaiden, I mean no disrespect, for I come bearing gifts for your fated," he told me, placing a hand on my arm and calming my Wrath just as he had the power to do. You see, the misconception of the ruler over Wrath's realms wasn't anger, it was the opposite. It was the power to absorb that hatred and that fury and use it against those that tried to use it as a weapon. It was the gift only my father held here, and it was why he would beat anyone angry enough to fight him. I may have been able to beat him, but one touch and he would take that fight right out of me with a single thought.

I was all of the rage of the King of Wrath.

*He was the calm that counteracted it.*

Which was why I let him go and took a step back, taking a breath like he silently commanded me to do.

"She calms your Wrath too, I can tell… a single touch, am I correct?" he asked with a raise of his brow.

"How did you know?"

"It is her gift, that and more no doubt, but you only discover that when she is granted back the power of a true Siren. Besides, she is fated to the Son of Wrath after all." At this I had to grin. "Unfortunate timing, I am sure, yet it cannot wait," he told me.

"Why not?"

"Because there is another Siren that calls for her Demon, Mammon has felt it calling out to his son." I reacted to this.

"You speak of Ryker Wyeth, Enforcer of Central Canada?" I questioned, knowing of the man well and his accumulating wealth, as was his nature. He was also a force to be reckoned with and not a Demon I would ever want as my enemy.

"Reach out to him, as his father believes his fate is now tied to that of your own."

"This could have waited!" I snapped, making him place a calming hand to my shoulder and tell me,

"No, it couldn't as fate waits for no man, my son. Now as for Dagon."

"I don't have time to talk about that fuck!" I growled.

"Then make time, as what I tell you now is important, and enough time has passed between now and the destiny that brought you into this hellish world." I scrubbed a frustrated hand down my face and asked,

"And how is any of this connected to my fate? How is Dagon connected to me at all!?" This was when my father dropped a Hell sized bombshell on me...

*"Because I am the one who took his daughter from him."*

⚜

The moment my father released his hold on me, I ended up back where I started, only now with one major difference...

*My Siren was gone.*

244

I quickly looked at the clock on the wall and growled in anger, knowing there was little wonder she wasn't here. I had been in Hell for hours, despite it only being minutes of my own time.

*"Fuck!"* I growled, knowing that she must be out of her mind with worry! Gods, all I could hope for was that she had remained at the mansion waiting for me. However, after calling forth my clothes, having no fucking time to change like a mortal, I bent down to pick up something calling to me. A scent I now craved... something coating my T-shirt. She had used it to clean herself as it was now covered with the dry remains of our claiming.

But why had she used this, as though in a hurry? Not that I cared she had, but I still questioned this instead of her taking a shower, one I would have expected her to take. No, something wasn't sitting right with me. For one, I couldn't feel her presence in my home, and I knew I had taken enough of her blood to do so. I should have felt her.

*But I didn't.*

I suddenly dropped the shirt and ran through the house, calling her name.

"Emmeline!" I called her over and over but there was nothing. In fact, there was no one here!

"Where the fuck is everyone!?" I shouted in my rage, having no choice but to run down to the lower levels. I needed to see if there was anything on the surveillance footage that suggested where she may be. I ignored the mess on the floor I had made when ripping one of the screens from the wall in my anger. This only now making me question how it came to be on there and more importantly, why had Franklin not seen it?

245

Had he been the one to falsify the video?

I had been so lost in my little Halo at the time, I hadn't even stopped to think of these things. I started tapping on keys, using the machinery to wind back the footage, seeing now that my brother had in fact, taken Emmeline somewhere. I took a deep, calming breath, knowing at least she was safe and no doubt at the club with him waiting for my return. Gods, but she had looked so panicked, I knew that I would have a lot of explaining to do when I got her back.

But my father had been right, what he had to tell me couldn't wait. Because long ago, my enemy Dagon had once been an enemy to my father first. This was after an imprisoned girl had escaped Dagon's clutches, a being who loved her not like a father should love his daughter but like an evil tyrant had loved a possession he owned and would abuse, calling it love. She had managed to escape him long enough to find herself in my father's realm seeking refuge.

He admitted to me, to falling in love with her against all odds of the King of Wrath loving anyone. This was the storm before my father's powers led to calm. I had never known any of this, for I believed my father's power born, not created by his love for another. It was how he knew about Emmeline and the power she too held over me.

*She was the calm to my own storm.*

This love was returned by the girl but after she gave birth to two Demonic souls in Hell, her body was curse by her father and could not survive in Hell any longer. My father had no choice but to send her soul to be reborn into the mortal world, until one day knowing that he would find her again and claim her for good. That he would one day...

*Claim back my mother.*

Which meant that in the cruellest twist of fate, I was the one who would be charged with sending Dagon back to the Hell. The one he was born from, and delivering him straight in the hands of my father so as he too could get his revenge.

*My grandfather, who would pay with his life.*

That was why Dagon had always blamed me and my brother for his daughter's death. We had been born and the result had been losing our mother's life.

"What the fuck is all this and why were their no guards at the gate?" my brother's voice dragged me from my father's past as he approached from behind me. I knew I would have to tell him all our father had said but that day was not this one.

"Where is Emmeline?!" I snapped, making him frown back at me.

"How the fuck should I know, I thought she would still be in your bed by now," he said, making my veins turn to ice. I grabbed him to me and roared,

"YOU TOOK HER!" At this he showed me his own Demon and hammered an arm down, breaking my hold with ease before telling me,

*"No... I didn't!"* I turned and pressed play on the footage and said,

"Then explain this to me?!" At this he shoved me out of the way and stared dumbfounded at the screen.

"That... that wasn't fucking me!" I swear his words felt like a knife across my skin.

"You have to believe me! I would never..." I took a deep breath and interrupted him.

"I know, my brother, for I also know when the truth

comes out of your lips," I said on a growl of pained frustration.

"What the fuck is going on and where is Emmeline?" he asked, and I snarled back at the screen and said,

"I don't know, but I will tell you something…

*"I will rip this whole fucking world apart until I find her!"*

## CHAPTER 32
# RYKER WYETH

The truth of events soon started to unfold after all the footage was found, and we had one person in particular questioned.

A bitch named...

*Raina.*

She was the key to all of this. I knew that after seeing footage of what actually transpired in the library that night. Not only had she been expressing her concerns of the plan not working, she had also orchestrated a way for me to suspect Emmeline of trying to run from me. Naturally, *I was fucking furious!*

Lucky for her, she was not within my grasp but thankfully, I knew people. Like, say, an Enforcer who ruled Australia and the very place where I had sent Raina. Unsurprisingly, they had found her trying to escape the country. It also transpired that she wasn't even mortal, but an Angel that had the ability to manipulate the feelings of others, along with masking how they appeared to even her own kind. She was a strong supernatural to be able to achieve this, for it was not an easy task being able to keep up that type of veil for such a length of time.

She didn't even look like the same fucking woman as she had! But this was not a surprise either, as she had to be close to her targets to weave her spell and keep it for a long time. It was why the 'snatch and grab' had been faked outside the club. An excuse to get closer to me to weave an even greater spell, making me feel what she had wanted me to. It had all been false.

But her plan hadn't worked.

A plan she had been working on for years. One that really came into play when she could steal the thoughts of Emmeline, taking the exact appearance of Raina straight out of her mind. She knew then that Emmeline suddenly seeing a woman she had dreamed about for the last six years would create enough doubt in her mind so as to not let me claim her. A plan she had been waiting to set into motion for years after reading her book, knowing that one day I would encounter my Siren. Of course, it also turned out that she was working for Dagon, at the same time working for me.

*A waitress named, Katina.*

The very same one that had knocked whiskey down Emmeline, getting cast out for the offence, just as she needed to be at the time so as not to be the cause for suspicion. It had all been staged. But she hadn't been working alone as it seemed Franklin also hadn't been who he seemed to be.

This was only discovered when I had his home broken into, hoping for another body to torture information from. However, what I found was a lot more than I bargained for, finding not only the cloak used to cover up the person who tried to kill my Siren. But also, what remained of Franklin's half eaten vessel.

Manushya-Rakshasi.

A shifter Demon that needed fresh mortal flesh to shift to another form. One that this time was to be none other than…

*My brother's.*

Thankfully, combined with Katina's confession, I had enough of an idea where to find my girl, which was why I was on a plane right now, heading to Central Canada.

We had managed to trace their movements enough to know a plane was hired, something I only realised after I had seen the list of all destinations from all privately chartered flights. And after speaking with my father about destiny and fate being now, it meant that only one place stood out.

*"Well, fuck me,"* I had muttered. Only explaining this to Hel once we were on our own plane, heading to the very place my father had told me where an Enforcer needed to meet his own Siren.

Which was why my next call had been made to another ruthless ruler…

*Ryker Wyeth.*

# CHAPTER 33
# SIRENS DROWNING
## EMMELINE

$\mathcal{I}$ *had been fooled.*

Something that admittedly had taken me far too long to figure out, say like a private flight all the way to Ontario, Canada. But then Hel's cold treatment of me I was putting down to his brother's worry and seeing as this matched my own, I spent most of the flight trying not to bother him. He spoke on the phone to someone for the most part, doing so in a language I didn't understand.

So, I had continued to look out the window, swiping at my silent tears asking myself over and over if Kaiden would be alright. Surely his father wouldn't hurt him, would he? I had no clue but continued to torture my mind with these types of questions for the duration.

That was until it was time to get off the plane.

That was until I saw a man I knew.

*Dagon Weaver.*

After this I hadn't even had time to make a single move to run, hearing only his arrogant greeting,

"We meet at last, *Wrath's Siren.*" Then he nodded to Hel

at my back, and I felt the chemically soaked cloth held firmly over my mouth and nose, giving me no option other than to eventually breathe in the fumes.

*After this I blacked out.*

However, the next time I woke I found myself in the very last place I thought to be…*in water.* I woke with a start and found half my body draped over a plastic rock with the other half of my body floating in water. I then shook the fog from my brain the best I could when I heard the desperate cries of another woman, calling for me.

"You need to wake up! Oh, please wake up." I started to move then, and her relief didn't go unheard.

"Oh thank God, you're not hurt." She said, a voice that was followed by the splashing sound of water as she was clearly trying to move closer. I looked around to find we were both in two separate tanks positioned next to each other. There was also a buzz of a crowd heard beyond a large curtain that had been used to cut off the view in front of us. Hiding our own enclosures like we were some kind of new creature about to be shown to the public in a zoo.

"Where are we?" I asked my voice groggy from being drugged.

"We are in a place called the London Psychiatric Hospital in Ontario. It looks like it has been abandoned for a long time. They dragged me in here, but you were already unconscious." She said and now I could focus on her, I saw that she, like me was wearing a long white dress, that was corseted at the top, fitted tight to our bodies. The skirts were left floating in the water, like the tails of a mermaid.

As for the girl, she had long dark brown hair plaited to one side and sweet freckled skin, with speckles across her nose and tops of her cheeks. Her eyes were a much lighter brown colour than my own and her body was slim and petite.

As for our tanks, they were about the size of a rectangular room, no bigger than ten ft by ten ft. They were made to try and resemble a small beach with sand on the floor and a single plastic rock we were both perched on. The entire thing was enclosed with bars above to prevent us from getting out. Thankfully the water wasn't too deep but anymore and I would have been freaking out as the tank was at least twelve feet tall!

"What do they want with us?" I asked the woman,

"I don't know, but whilst I have been held captive, I've heard people talking about an auction." She told me holding herself around the waist shivering and she wasn't the only one, as the water was fucking cold.

But before we could say anymore to each other there was a booming voice demanding silence from the room.

"Silence! Welcome ladies and gentlemen. We start this year's auction with the long-awaited treasures of Heaven, I give you two of the Lost Sirens!" After this a curtain was dropped and I gasped at the sight of the huge crowd, all seated in luxury seating but surrounded by a decaying building. However, my own cry of shock was drowned out by the sound of the whole room reacting as one, gasping together.

Large broken windows, smashed or completely missing from their frames surrounded both sides of the hall we were now situated in. Daylight flooded in, telling me I had been gone at least a day. Broken floor boards, many bent and twisted had been ripped up in sections but the space could still be used for the vast amounts of chairs. Each one with a person occupying them, no doubt ready to bid. I knew that thanks to the numbered paddles they held at the ready in their laps.

Most of the crowd looked dressed in their best, with some others dotted around looking more ready for action. Was this the events security?

"Oh shit." The other woman said making me want to offer her some comfort.

"It's okay, we will be okay." She nodded trying to stay brave, something that ended as soon as the man behind the mic, a person we couldn't see as they were raise up behind us on a platform, started to speak again.

"Let's make this more interesting should we, Randel, if you please." Seconds later and the pretty woman next to me began to panic, as the water in her tank started to rise dramatically.

"No! Stop…stop this!" I shouted for her as she started to bang her fist against the sides of the tank. She tried to pull herself out of the way of the rising water only to realize that even stood on the rock, wouldn't make you high enough to get away from the rising water level.

"I can't fucking swim!" she shouted making me gasp! However, the guy on the mic just laughed,

"This particular Siren is brought to you by our esteemed vendor Gastian, one of the Kings own Enforcers. Should we start the bidding at one million!" he said making the girl's mouth drop,

*"No way"* then she started banging harder, crying out when her foot slipped. I watched her fall, scrambling against the rock to try and keep her head out of the water. She managed it back on, now gaining her footing once more.

"Someone save her, for fuck sake!" I screamed, when the water was up to her neck. She was trying to stand as tall as she could after climbing on the plastic rock, holding her head up when suddenly she screamed, crying out,

"HELP ME!" after this a handsome man stood and shouted his own bid,

*"One hundred million!"*

"SOLD!" the auctioneer shouted but as for the man that had bid, he was already on the move knowing he would win with this kind of money. Which meant he was already storming his long legs down the center aisle, and just as the girls' head went under, he leapt to the top of her tank like some kind of demonic jungle cat, morphing from a beast back into a man!

He then ripped off the barred latch above and reached inside as she too was reaching her hand up to him. He then pulled her from the water and gathered her up in his arms. Then he jumped down with her now soaking wet and curled up against his large chest. The guy was a beast, being almost as big as Kaiden.

I didn't have much chance at seeing more as it was soon my turn, as the water started to fill my tank, making me panic this time.

"This next Siren comes to us by a new vendor, Dagon Weaver brings us this beautiful Siren. One he assures me is not yet claimed just like the last Siren as is stated on your catalogs. So, the price should again reflect that. So, let's start this off at ten million this time!" he said getting bids straight away as the water line rose quicker this time. I ended up doing the same as the girl, standing on the rock and looking to where Hel now appeared, stood with his arms folded watching the whole thing play out.

"Why are you doing this!" I cried out unable to believe he had been a traitor to his brother all this time. It was beyond heartbreaking!

"Someone please!" I shouted just as the water was about to cover my head. But then I heard an almighty roar that actually managed to crack the sides of the tank I was imprisoned inside. Water sprayed out the largest of these lightning bolts marring the glass.

Suddenly a Demonic presence appeared from the back of the room and the second I saw who it was, I mouthed his name under the water, seeing my savor just in time.

'Kaiden'

He released his wings making everyone in the room gasp at the sight, as he flew straight over to me and the second he landed, he hammered a fist into the biggest crack. This made the tank smash instantly and as water poured out, I went right out with it, quickly caught in Kaiden's arms as I did. The rest of the crowd scattered as the water poured out all around them, putting a wet end to the auction before it had really even begun.

"My Siren." Kaiden whispered down at me, lifting me up so as he could kiss me gently.

"You know the law, she is to be sold, so release her or pay…"

"She is a Siren already claimed and therefore your vendor's sale is null and void!" Hel shouted making me frown in confusion as he suddenly appeared from behind the man that looked the spitting imagine of him! Then without a word of warning, he grabbed the man from behind and with total bad ass style ease, he snapped his neck like a twig and dropped his dead body to the floor.

But then just as I started to close my eyes, exhausted from my ordeal, Kaiden's voice brought me home, along with his words of comfort,

"Time to take you home, little Halo, *once and for all.*" Kaiden then held me tighter in his arms and walked me straight from this Hellish place,

Now taking…

*His Claimed Siren Home.*

## CHAPTER 34
# HELL'S BLESSING
### WRATH

A WEEK LATER

"Where is she!" I growled storming out of the room she should have been in only to find her gone. I swear but she was going to make me fucking grey, as I was beyond the fucking fear of finding her missing! I was straight at fucking furious!

"Whoa okay before you tear down the fucking house, she wanted me to give you this." My brother said the moment he turned a corner, obviously on his way to see me and now I knew why.

"What the fuck is this?!" I snapped making my brother smirk,

"I don't know Brother, but it looks like a note to me."

"I know it's a fucking note!"

"Then now we have that confusion cleared up, may I suggest reading it and finding out." Hel said making me narrow my gaze at him before doing so at the folded paper in my hand.

"Look, just go with it okay." He added hitting me on the side of my arm and granting me a wink before walking off. So, I did just that and unfolded the paper, that said only one thing,

*'You will find me in our room*
*Oh, and don't worry, I've already got the chains.'*

I chuckled at this and was still doing so as I took off running. My naughty little Siren obviously had a plan to recreate what we had once started down in the interrogation room. I swear I was fucking grinning from ear to ear by the time I got there. However, the moment I opened the door to the room, I swear my heart stopped fucking beating!

This was because the gorgeous sight before me was her wearing nothing but the cutest, fucking sexiest, black babydoll lingerie dress that I had ever seen, one covered in reed hearts of all things! Oh, and that wasn't all, as this time she was wearing black leather cuffs on each wrist, chained in the middle and a pair far too flimsy to be taken seriously. However, she still managed to achieve the impact she was clearly going for, as my cock was rock hard in seconds!

"Hey, there's my sexy Enforcer," she teased with red painted lips making this my new private mission, for how long it would take me to kiss them free of the colour.

Because her hair was already as she knew I loved to see it, down, wild and free and ready for my hand.

However, as I walked in there, already taking off my jacket, ready to take her on the fucking table, one I had been seconds away from taking her virginity on, she stopped me dead. This was as she opened a hand and showed me a single box in black velvet waiting there.

"I know this isn't how it's usually done, but then again, we aren't exactly your poster couple for typical written love stories." She teased chuckling but even through this I could see that she was nervous.

"I got you something, erm…Hel helped of course, starting with giving me back my bank cards." She told me as I approached slowly, now unable to take my eyes from that little box in her hands. However, the second she shifted from the table and started to drop to her knees, I noticed the small cushion there.

"I came prepared." She told me but I swear my mind wouldn't fucking work, now just looking down at her sat before me. My Siren, on her knees and holding out her hands to me before she opened the box. Then she asked me the very last thing I ever expected.

*"Will you marry me Kaiden Wrath?"* and this was when my brain and my body finally kicked into gear moving as one. I dropped to my knees before her, took her face in my hands and kissed her, giving her the only answer she would need. Yet still,

My words followed,

"Only if you marry me back, *Siren of mine.*" I said pulling my own ring from my pocket and one that had been

263

given to me to gift to my Siren from my father. A ring he had once given to my mother.

Then with tears still in her eyes at seeing my own ring held out to her,

I told her…

*"My Father sends his blessing."*

# EPILOGUE
## WRATH

*WEEKS LATER...*

I looked down at my ring, as was my usual habit these days, reading the inscription engraved on my black ring, gifted to me by my wife.

My love and now, *my entire reason for living.*

My Siren.

The words I read there, always made me smile,

> *'My Love Forever and Eternity, your Siren.*
> *Emmeline.'*

Gods but how I loved her, with my obsession only growing stronger by the day. She lived with me now and no longer behind locked doors. Although in truth this had taken a while for me to get out of the habit. Something she would chuckle at when hearing the lock of our door at night.

But as I sat waiting for my King to arrive, I also had to think of the fate of my brother, knowing what was coming.

As for my trip to Hell, I had told him about our father's admission, knowing now that our mother was out there somewhere in the world. That one day, fate would bring us all together again. But it was more than this, as I knew what my King was about to require in exchange for this meeting. Something I had yet to even discuss with my brother.

*He would not be happy.*

As for Raina, whose identity was actually Katina, she had also been punished. She almost begged for the Enforcer who tortured the truth from her, to end her life. Especially after she had confessed to being the one that tried to kill Emmeline, by pushing her off the balcony in her jealousy. Despite this not being as Dagon planned, as he had always intended to sell her off to make me pay and suffer. However, he had no idea that I had already claimed her, making whatever contract he had for sale, null and void. As for the shifter demon, Hel had made short work killing him and sending him back to where he belonged.

"Kaiden Wrath" Dominic Draven said my name making me stand in his presence. The King of Kings was nearly as tall as I was and just as wide. He was also as he was usually seen, wearing a full suit, creating that masterful presence of a man that had ruled the world for thousands of years.

But he was also a man that had my respect, for he was a good King who ruled fairly yet with an iron fist for those that ever defied him.

"My lord, King." I replied with a bow of my head, rising from the seat in his office.

"You will be happy to hear I found you a late wedding gift." I smirked at this as a bloody and beaten man was dragged in by his head of security Ragnar. A Devourer demon who was bigger than both of us and one hard mother fucker to kill!

"I hope it doesn't take the pleasure out of this, but I found myself eager to add some of my own justice. I'm sure you understand." I bowed my head again and told him,

"A prolonged misery with a beating by his King would never take away from the experience." I told him as Dagon was thrown at my feet before Ragnar left the room without a word.

"But I am an Enforcer, you cannot kill me! I demand a trial my Lord!" he shouted, making Dominic Draven laugh, a fucking scary and chilling sound at that.

"But your life is not your own for I had it bargained for." The King replied with his own deadly smirk,

"My Lord?" Dagon enquired but it was my turn to answer him, as I grabbed his hair and wretched his head back,

"The King owes me a life dept and well, I am here to claim it, for there was only one life I could think of I wanted in return...*Yours Asshole!*" I snarled, before bringing forth my demon's hand and slicing my claws across his throat.

*"Say hello to my father, won't you!"*

He didn't even get chance to scream as I cut straight through the vocal cords, making him fall forward as he bled to the stone floor.

"You know what this means." The King said barely sparing a glance at his once Enforcer now bleeding all over his office floor.

"I will inform my brother of his new position shortly."

"Do you think he will resist?" he asked with a knowing grin.

"My brother? Undoubtably, but I agree, there is no one better to take over this shit stains sector. Helmer will not deny you, my Lord."

"Excellent, then I will leave the details to you, for I have far more important matters to deal with." He said looking at his watch making me ask,

"Your fated, my Lord?" At this he really grinned and for once, it wasn't the evil sinister one I was used to seeing. Oh yeah, the King was no doubt as obsessed with his Electus as I was with my Siren.

"My Keira will be here shortly, but I have to say that I am surprised and perhaps a little disappointed, as I thought you would make it last, Wrath Demon." My King said glancing at the dying man on the floor I was about to send as a gift to my father. But I shrugged my shoulders and told him,

*I have a Siren to get home to.*

The End.

# ACKNOWLEDGEMENTS

Well first and foremost my love goes out to all the people who deserve the most thanks which is you the FANS!

Without you wonderful people in my life, I would most likely still be serving burgers and writing in my spare time like some dirty little secret, with no chance to share my stories with the world.

You enable me to continue living out my dreams every day and for that I will be eternally grateful to each and every one of you!

Your support is never ending. Your trust in me and the story is never failing. But more than that, your love for me and all who you consider your 'Afterlife family' is to be commended, treasured and admired. Thank you just doesn't seem enough, so one day I hope to meet you all and buy you all a drink! ;)

To my family...

To my crazy mother, who had believed in me since the beginning and doesn't think that something great should be hidden from the world. I would like to thank you for all the hard work you put into my books and the endless hours spent caring about my words and making sure it is the best it can be for everyone to enjoy. You, along with the Hudson Indie Ink team make Afterlife shine.

To my crazy father who is and always has been my hero in life. Your strength astonishes me, even to this day! The love and care you hold for your family is a gift you give to the Hudson name.

To my lovely sister,

If Peter Pan had a female version, it would be you and Wendy combined. You have always been my big, little sister and another person in my life that has always believed me capable of doing great things. You were the one who gave Afterlife its first identity and I am honored to say that you continue to do so even today. We always dreamed of being able to work together and I am thrilled that we made it happened when you agreed to work as a designer at Hudson Indie Ink.

And last but not least, to the man that I consider my soul mate. The man who taught me about real love and makes me not only want to be a better person but makes me feel I am too. The amount of support you have given me since we met has been incredible and the greatest feeling was finding out you wanted to spend the rest of your life with me when you asked me to marry you.

All my love to my dear husband and my own personal Draven… Mr Blake Hudson.

To My Team…

I am so fortunate enough to rightly state the claim that I have the best team in the world!

It is a rare thing indeed to say that not a single person

that works for Hudson Indie Ink doesn't feel like family, but there you have it. We Are a Family.

Sarah your editing is a stroke of genius and you, like others in my team, work incredibly hard to make the Afterlife world what it was always meant to be. But your personality is an utter joy to experience and getting to be a part of your crazy feels like a gift.

Sloane, it is an honor to call you friend and have you not only working for Hudson Indie Ink but also to have such a talented Author represented by us. Your formatting is flawless and makes my books look more polished than ever before.

Xen, your artwork is always a masterpiece that blows me away and again, I am lucky to have you not only a valued member of my team but also as another talented Author represented by Hudson Indie Ink.

Lisa, my social media butterfly and count down Queen! I was so happy when you accepted to work with us, as I knew you would fit in perfectly with our family! Please know you are a dear friend to me and are a such an asset to the team. Plus, your backward dancing is the stuff of legends!

Libby, as our newest member of the team but someone I consider one of my oldest and dearest friends, you came in like a whirlwind of ideas and totally blew me away with your level of energy! You fit in instantly and I honestly don't know what Hudson Indie Ink would do without you. What you have achieved in such a short time is utterly incredible and want you to know you are such an asset to the team!

And last but by certainly not least is the wonderful Claire, my right-hand woman! I honestly have nightmares about waking one day and finding you not working for

Hudson Indie Ink. You are the backbone of the company and without you and all your dedicated, hard work, there would honestly be no Hudson Indie Ink!

You have stuck by me for years, starting as a fan and quickly becoming one of my best friends. You have supported me for years and without fail have had my back through thick and thin, the ups and the downs. I could quite honestly write a book on how much you do and how lost I would be without you in my life!

I love you honey x

Thanks to all of my team for the hard work and devotion to the saga and myself. And always going that extra mile, pushing Afterlife into the spotlight you think it deserves. Basically helping me achieve my secret goal of world domination one day...evil laugh time... Mwahaha! Joking of course ;)

Another personal thank you goes to my dear friend Caroline Fairbairn and her wonderful family that have embraced my brand of crazy into their lives and given it a hug when most needed.

For their friendship I will forever be eternally grateful.

As before, a big shout has to go to all my wonderful fans who make it their mission to spread the Afterlife word and always go the extra mile. Those that have remained my fans all these years and supported me, my Afterlife family, you also meant the world to me.

All my eternal love and gratitude,
Stephanie x

# ABOUT THE AUTHOR

Stephanie Hudson has dreamed of being a writer ever since her obsession with reading books at an early age. What first became a quest to overcome the boundaries set against her in the form of dyslexia has turned into a life's dream. She first started writing in the form of poetry and soon found a taste for horror and romance. Afterlife is her first book in the series of twelve, with the story of Keira and Draven becoming ever more complicated in a world that sets them miles apart.

When not writing, Stephanie enjoys spending time with her loving family and friends, chatting for hours with her biggest fan, her sister Cathy who is utterly obsessed with one gorgeous Dominic Draven. And of course, spending as much time with her supportive partner and personal muse, Blake who is there for her no matter what.

**Author's words.**

My love and devotion is to all my wonderful fans that keep me going into the wee hours of the night but foremost to my wonderful daughter Ava...who yes, is named after a cool, kick-ass, Demonic bird and my sons, Jack, who is a little hero and Baby Halen, who yes, keeps me up at night but it's okay because he is named after a Guitar legend!

**Keep updated with all new release news & more on my website**
www.afterlifesaga.com
Never miss out, sign up to the
mailing list at the website.

Also, please feel free to join myself and other Dravenites on
my Facebook group
Afterlife Saga Official Fan
Interact with me and other fans. Can't wait to see you there!

facebook.com/AfterlifeSaga

twitter.com/afterlifesaga

instagram.com/theafterlifesaga

# ALSO BY STEPHANIE HUDSON

**Afterlife Saga**

*Afterlife*

*The Two Kings*

*The Triple Goddess*

*The Quarter Moon*

*The Pentagram Child - Part 1*

*The Pentagram Child - Part 2*

*The Cult of the Hexad*

*Sacrifice of the Septimus - Part 1*

*Sacrifice of the Septimus - Part 2*

*Blood of the Infinity War*

*Happy Ever Afterlife - Part 1*

*Happy Ever Afterlife - Part 2*

*The Forbidden Chapters*

\*

**Transfusion Saga**

*Transfusion*

*Venom of God*

*Blood of Kings*

*Rise of Ashes*

*Map of Sorrows*

*Tree of Souls*

*Kingdoms of Hell*

*Eyes of Crimson*

*Roots of Rage*

*Heart of Darkness*

*Wraith of Fire*

*Queen of Sins*

\*

King of Kings

*Dravens Afterlife*

*Dravens Electus*

\*

Kings of Afterlife

*Vincent's Immortal Curse*

*The Hellbeast King*

*The Hellbeast's Fight*

*The Hellbeast's Mistake*

\*

The Shadow Imp Series

*Imp and the Beast*

*Beast and the Imp*

\*

The Lost Siren Series

*Ward's Siren*

*Eden's Enforcer*

*Wrath's Siren*

*Emme's Enforcer*

\*

Afterlife Academy: (Young Adult Series)

*The Glass Dagger*

*The Hells Ring*

*The Reapers*

\*

Stephanie Hudson and Blake Hudson

*The Devil in Me*

# OTHER AUTHORS AT HUDSON INDIE INK

**Paranormal Romance/Urban Fantasy**

Sloane Murphy

Xen Randell

C. L. Monaghan

Sorcha Dawn

Kia Carrington-Russell

**Sci-fi/Fantasy**

Devin Hanson

**Crime/Action**

Blake Hudson

Mike Gomes

**Contemporary Romance**

Gemma Weir